The Protector

ALSO BY DAN LATUS

FRANK DOY SERIES
Book 1: Risky Mission
Book 2: Out Of The Night
Book 3: A Death At South Gare
Book 4: Living Dangerously
Book 5: One Damn Thing After Another
Book 6: Saving Harry
Book 7:Borovksy's Gold
Book 8: Terror From The Sea
Book 9: Not Dead Yet
Book 10: The Hitman's Assassin
Book 11: Playing Dirty
Book 12: The Protector

JAKE ORD THRILLERS
Book 1: No Place To Hide
Book 2: Never Look Back
Book 3: Last Resort

STANDALONES
Run For Home
And Then You're Dead

THE PROTECTOR

DAN LATUS

Frank Doy Book 12

Joffe Books, London
www.joffebooks.com

First published in Great Britain in 2025

© Dan Latus

Cover art by Nebojša Zorić

ISBN: 978-1-83526-981-7

For Sandra, with love

CHAPTER ONE

Haverton Hill, Teesside
15 April

There were six men present, standing in the poor light of late afternoon in two opposing groups of three. One of the men, dressed in a formal dark suit, spoke to the three before him.

'And that's your final answer, is it? No chance of you guys changing your minds?'

All around them, water dripped from the broken pipes and ruined structures of what had once been a powerful oil rig standing proud more than a hundred miles out in the North Sea. Wind that had followed the river upstream from the sea shrieked through the tangle of wrecked metalwork high above the men. Somewhere a generator throbbed. Somewhere, what sounded like a steam hammer pounded.

The younger of the two men standing alongside the speaker paid little attention to the discussion. He didn't like it here, in this cavernous, filthy shell, and couldn't wait to get out. He resented having to be here, even. What was going on with the three divers was nothing to do with him. He had no idea why the boss had demanded his presence.

Instead of the talk, he listened to the drip-drip-drip of leaking water finding its way through a structure that once had housed two-hundred men. He heard the creak and clang of tortured metal, and the moaning of the wind. He smelled the salty odour and the oil fumes wafting off corroded metal that had spent long decades at sea and now, at last, was back on land again.

The oldest of the three divers, their spokesman, said in a bleak tone, 'What you're doing is wrong. What you want us to do is wrong. We want no part of it.'

'Not even for the extra money I'm offering you?'

'We've told you. We're done here.'

'No chance of changing your minds?'

The diver now spoke with contempt. 'We don't work for you anymore. We've quit.'

That was the moment the younger man sensed something change. With a start, his attention switched fully back to the meeting.

There was a brief moment of calm. Then the boss nodded to the older man to his other side. They both pulled out guns and shot the three divers. Shot them repeatedly, until it was certain they were all dead.

The younger man was startled and shocked. But he had heard gunfire before. His reflexes took over and instinctively he did what he had once been trained to do. He ran for cover, and found it temporarily behind a pile of junk metal.

'Get back here!' the boss called after him. 'Give Smith a hand to get rid of the bodies.'

'No way! What the hell did you do that for?'

'You're either with us, Burke, or you're not. What's it going to be?'

The younger man didn't hesitate. He was wide awake and fully engaged now, his shock under control. He had been in war zones before and he knew without thinking what to do. The next few seconds were vital, and his current position was untenable.

He trusted to speed and luck, and ran for better cover.

CHAPTER TWO

It was one of those dark, still November days when I heard it. Late afternoon. Dusk. Misty. The tide almost on the full, but the sea calm. Only the gulls disturbing the quiet until I heard that distinctive sound. Faint at first, but it grew quickly and soon began to reverberate all around me.

I was standing on the tiny patch of shingle on the beach at the foot of the cliffs below Risky Point, where I live in Cleveland. I'd been working on *Fair Lady*, the coble that Jimmy Mack and I kept down there, and I was about finished. All I had in mind now was to gather up my tools and make my way back up the cliff path to the cottage, before it got dark.

The coble actually belonged to Jimmy, a fisherman by trade and my only neighbour. But it was me that used it most these days, and I did most of the maintenance work on it now. Jimmy's arthritis meant it had become a real struggle for him to get up and down the cliff. So, apart from the occasional excursion, his fishing days in *Fair Lady* were over, sadly.

That was how things stood when I first heard the engine noise from something small with a very powerful motor. Definitely not another coble, with the familiar put-put sound of a two-stroke engine. This sounded more like a RIB, a rigid inflatable boat, something fast and lightweight: a power boat. I couldn't see anything out there in the mist, but I was pretty sure that was what it was. I wondered what it was doing, so close inshore, and getting closer.

Coming this way? Surely not?

But it was.

The engine noise kept on growing until the slim black shape of a RIB swept out of the mist. It was travelling at speed, and the roar of the engine didn't let up until it was no more than fifty yards from the beach. Even then, the boat kept on coming.

I couldn't begin to guess what the two-man crew were thinking, never mind intending. This was nowhere. There was nothing here for them, nothing at all. Yet emerging from the mist and seeing the beach didn't make them realise they had made a mistake and turn away. They continued heading towards the shore, in as straight a line as a draughtsman might have drawn on his drafting table. All I could do was watch, and wonder.

The RIB came right on in until it grounded on the shingle. Then, with the engine noise no more than a low rumble now, the crew leapt out into the knee-deep water.

'You!' one of them shouted, beckoning at me. 'Come with us.'

I grinned, more than a little surprised. 'Go with you?'

'Now!' he ordered.

'What are you talking about?'

'Come — now!'

'I really don't think so,' I told him, annoyed. 'Who the hell are you anyway?'

A pistol appeared in his hand. He pointed it at me. Things had got serious, and fast.

'In the boat!'

4

Meanwhile, his buddy had circled round behind me. Glancing round, I saw that he, too, had a gun in hand. He prodded me with it, urging me forward.

I couldn't believe this. But I couldn't ignore it either. They looked like they knew what they were doing, and they were very serious about it.

For a moment, a very brief one, I considered lashing out and making a fight of it. Good sense put a stop to that. Risking being shot was not a sensible option to take at this stage.

I got in the boat.

CHAPTER THREE

Neither man spoke to me again on the way out to sea. I did try speaking to them, asking where we were going, why they wanted me and so on, but I met a blank stone wall.

It was far too noisy and generally uncomfortable anyway for sustained conversation. The roar of the engine, the spray, and the bouncing up and down all made for a high-speed journey that would have been unpleasant even without my growing apprehension about my prospects. I had avoided death on the beach, perhaps, but for how long would my good fortune last?

What about my abductors? Who were they? Whose orders were they following? I ran through the possibilities as we travelled. It wasn't an easy or quick scan. Given what I do for a living — security consultant, bodyguard and occasional PI — it's long been likely there are plenty of people out there looking for payback, some foreign, others more local.

Foreign seemed to be the case here. The men who had come for me were not native Brits, although that didn't mean their boss wasn't. They were probably part of some criminal gang. That was my best bet. Not an insight of much comfort. More pressingly, I wondered what they wanted of me, and what the chances were of surviving the encounter.

The only time I could think of that came close to this experience was when rival salvage companies wanted my knowledge to aid their search for Borovsky's gold, the treasure supposedly lost in an oligarch's sunken yacht. That hadn't gone terribly well. A gold hoard hadn't been found, but at least I'd survived. Surely it couldn't be about that all over again?

All in all, it was a miserable, worrying journey. At first, I wondered if they were taking me somewhere along the coast or to a mother ship parked offshore. After five or ten minutes, I was in no doubt at all. I could rule out a landing. We were heading straight out to sea. The guy doing the steering made sure of that, never allowing the boat to deviate a fraction from a northerly bearing. His pal sat, keeping an eye on me, with gun ready.

Given that we were making for deeper water, it looked like the journey would end at a vessel of significant size, that was reluctant or unable to venture closer inshore. And all I could do about it was sit tight and hope for the best.

Jumping overboard wasn't an option. I reckoned we were a good five miles offshore by then, which was too far for me to swim even if the water had been warmer. A few years ago I'd once swum half a mile in this sea out of necessity, and had been lucky to survive. I couldn't imagine ever doing that again, never mind the distance we had just travelled.

The engine noise abated. We slowed. Less sea washed over the front of the boat. I strained my eyes, looking into the wall of what was now fog rather than mist, and in moments, became aware of something big and dark not very far ahead. The image grew stronger as we drifted, rather than powered, towards it. Obviously a ship of some size.

A voice hailed us in a language I didn't understand. Our man at the helm answered and got to his feet. The guy watching me relaxed. Seemingly, we had arrived.

CHAPTER FOUR

It was a trawler, a big one. A vessel capable of deep-sea voyages, not just pottering about among the inshore fisheries. The RIB pilot climbed aboard, helped by a crewman on the trawler. My guard motioned to me to follow suit. I hesitated, but not for long. A jab with his gun got me moving.

I'd long ago realised that most of us will do almost anything to prolong our own life, and I'm no exception. I clung to the thought that maybe I could explain to whoever was in charge how much of a mistake they were making, and how badly they had got the wrong man. Of what possible interest could I be to them?

But I didn't delude myself into thinking that what I said would make any difference. They hadn't gone to all this trouble for no reason, and probably hadn't made a mistake, either. For some reason, they wanted me. And now they'd got me.

I was the one who had made a mistake, it seemed. I should have put up a fight on the beach. Going down fighting would have been a better end than what I feared I might be facing here.

Urged and prodded on, I climbed the ladder. Then I was steered towards the bridge, the command centre of the ship. There, I experienced another shock — if anything, even greater than the one I'd experienced on the beach.

CHAPTER FIVE

I simply couldn't believe it at first. A familiar figure broke away from a conference over maps or charts with two other men and turned to greet me with a broad smile.

'Frank! You made it. Welcome aboard!'

I stared, at first with astonishment and then with mounting relief. After that came anger, fury even. I was looking at a man I had long considered a friend.

'What the hell's going on?' I snapped, sagging back against a bulkhead.

'Surprised, eh?'

Leon Podolsky chuckled, obviously greatly amused, delighted even.

'Surprised?' I shook my head and glared at him. 'What the hell is this, Leon? Your idea of a joke?'

'No joke. I just wanted to see you, Frank. There's a job I would like you to consider doing for me. And as I was passing through the area . . .'

'And that's why I've been abducted and dragged here at gunpoint? Not good enough, Leon!'

He frowned and looked perplexed. 'At gunpoint? What do you mean? I sent a boat to bring—'

I interrupted to give him a brief account of what had happened, and what my experience had been like. At least he heard me out, even if the cheery smile with which he had greeted me was soon replaced by a stony expression.

When I paused for a moment, breathless, he turned to the two men who had brought me and barked out a couple of questions. After they had answered him, he laid into them with a few short, blistering remarks that made them hang their heads. Then he dismissed them with a contemptuous expression and a wave of his arm.

'Stupid, stupid, stupid!' he snapped, turning back to me. 'They are so stupid. Fishermen! They know how to handle boats and catch fish, but that is all.'

He clasped a hand to his forehead and appealed to me for forgiveness.

'I am so sorry, Frank. It is my fault. I told them to find you, and that it was very important. But they knew nothing else, and they misunderstood. I forgot how they are. Where they come from. There, if the boss says it is urgent, they jump. So it is my fault. I didn't think of that. How can I ever apologise for what happened?'

I was in no mood for that, or for civilised conversation, to be honest. The limits of friendship had been reached, breached even. I sat down heavily on a nearby stool and waved off his apology and further explanation. All I wanted was to be returned to Risky Point as fast as possible.

'Can I tell you about the job I have in mind for you?' Leon asked.

I shook my head. 'I'm not interested. I'm busy. At least, I was. Just get me home.'

He considered for a moment and then nodded, probably realising I was in no mood to listen to anything more he had to say. Then he recalled the RIB crew, apologised to me again and wished me well. That was that. I left the trawler.

The journey back to Risky Point was every bit as fast and uncomfortable as the journey out had been, with one exception: a big one. I was no longer in fear of what might lie ahead.

The two crewmen got me ashore. Then the one who had held a gun on me all the way out looked me in the eye and said, 'You friend, huh? Podolsky friend?'

'That's right.'

'Sorry,' he said, holding out a hand for me to shake.

Reluctantly, I took it.

'We not know,' he added.

I just nodded.

Then the skipper wanted to shake my hand, as well.

After that they turned the boat round and set off back out to sea. I watched until they disappeared into the mist, and listened to the sound of their retreating engine for a few moments more, before turning to make my way up the cliff path.

By now, it was fully dark. The climb was no easier than usual, which is to say not easy at all, but for once I scarcely noticed. I couldn't wait to get home.

CHAPTER SIX

Jimmy Mack was waiting for me when I got to the top of the cliff.

'Where've you been?' he asked.

'Out,' I said shortly, in no mood for chit-chat.

'What was all that about?' he asked with a chuckle.

I sighed and shook my head. 'You saw what happened, did you?'

'Some of it. I saw you going off in the boat, and I hoped I would see you coming back again. I can't do the work on *Fair Lady* myself these days.'

'It was Podolsky business,' I told him.

He nodded and looked thoughtful. 'That's all right, then,' he said dubiously.

Jimmy knew a bit about my relationship with the Podolsky family, but I didn't want to enlighten him further about what had just happened. It wasn't the time, and I wasn't in the mood. But I had to say something in case he'd realised I was forcibly abducted.

'Leon's out there,' I said.

'What? On a ship?'

I nodded.

'Leon, eh?' he said now with an approving chuckle. 'He certainly gets around, that man.'

I nodded and added, 'He wanted to see me.'

'Funny way of going about it.'

I managed a grin and said, 'He doesn't like it if you tell him no!'

Jimmy cackled with delight. 'You'd better not do that too often, then! But he's a good man, Leon.'

* * *

Later that evening, Bill Peart called round to see me. He's a pal, as well as being a DI in Cleveland Police. Sometimes, to his dismay and irritation, I find dead bodies he has to investigate. And sometimes we go fishing together. When he turns up unexpectedly, it's always a toss-up whether he's come for business or pleasure.

'Bill! Come on in. Haven't seen you for a while. How are you doing?'

'Not bad. I've been better, but I'm sure we could all say that.'

'You're telling me!'

I managed to desist from sharing what had happened to me a few hours earlier. I didn't want him going official on me and wondering if he should arrest Leon.

'Beer?' I asked.

'I wouldn't mind. And maybe some of that whisky Jimmy Mack likes so much.'

While I opened the cupboard and sought the whisky bottle, Bill got a couple of bottles of *Staropramen*, a Czech beer I like, from the fridge. I don't care for whisky, and almost never touch it, but Bill knows I keep a bottle that Jimmy likes to sample when he's feeling down, or up — or at any time, really. I wondered if Bill was feeling stressed about something.

I guessed he was planning, hoping at least, to make a night of it. He wouldn't be drinking at all if he was on duty, and he wouldn't be drinking beer and whisky if he was intending driving home. There are times when it feels like I'm running a seaside B&B, or maybe a bar. Something, anyway, for folks that want to get away from it all.

I put another driftwood log in the stove and allowed myself to collapse into the armchair to its side, Bill already occupying its companion on the other side.

'Done any fishing lately?' he asked.

'Not for a while, no. Been busy. But this afternoon I was down there, doing some work on the coble, and I began to think we ought to give it a go again. Do you fancy getting the boat out one of these days?'

'If it's not too rough, I wouldn't mind. A heavy sea, and I'd rather be on Skinningrove Pier.'

'Me an' all! But conditions are pretty good right now. We should think about it.'

'In a few days' time, maybe. I'm a bit stretched right now.'

'Oh?'

'The chief constable has a problem, and in his wisdom, he's wished it on me.'

Bill frowned for a moment before adding, 'Or the commissioner has. I'm never sure these days where these things start. There's so much politics involved. I just know where it all usually ends up.'

'So you've been lumbered with it?'

'I have,' he said with a sigh. 'Not that that's anything out of the ordinary. I'm used to getting the jobs no one else will do, or else will make sure they cock up to avoid being asked again.'

'You old cynic!'

But I knew there was some truth in what Bill was saying. He was no young high-flier. He was more of an old plodder, but a conscientious old plodder who would stick at it until he got some sort of resolution. There's a lot to be said for folk like that in all walks of life. Once upon a time, I aspired to be one myself.

'We're supposed to be keeping an eye on, looking out for, whatever you want to call it, a feller in Loftus who was in Witness Protection somewhere remote, but got tired of it and came back home.'

I put my beer bottle down carefully, wondering where this was going. What Bill had just said couldn't apply to very many people in Loftus, and only recently I had met one to whom it did.

'How are you planning to do that?' I asked innocently, playing for time while I tried to work out what I was prepared to tell him, if anything.

'Dunno,' Bill said heavily. 'It only got passed over to me today. I'm still thinking about it. Actually, I wondered if you might have anything to suggest.'

He glanced at me, and then, when I shook my head, back at the flames dancing behind the glass in the stove.

'It gives a good heat, that stove, doesn't it?' he remarked. 'Better than what we have in our house. Bloody boiler's on the blink again. I'm sick of calling out the repair man. He just says we need a new boiler.'

'Ah! So that's why you've come tonight? You were feeling the cold?'

He grinned. 'Well . . . that, and because the wife's staying at her sister's for a few days.'

'Fallen out with her, have you, the wife?'

He shook his head. 'It's not like that. Eileen, the sister, isn't too well these days. She's been in and out of hospital a few times. At the moment, she's back home again, but not much better.'

'What's wrong with her?'

'Supposed to be this Long Covid. You heard of that?'

'Not really. What is it?'

'Well, some folk that got Covid when it was all the rage survived, recovered even, but they still have some of the symptoms. Eileen's like that. She's just very tired, and feeling poorly all the time. So Mary's gone to look after her for a bit.'

'Nice of her. Doesn't Eileen have a husband to do that?'

'Not anymore. Bert died the other year — of Covid, actually.'

I winced and said I was sorry to hear it.

'Some people are just unlucky,' Bill concluded. 'Like that guy we're supposed to be looking out for, but who I doubt can be helped — not by us, anyway.'

'Who is he?'

'Feller called Jamie Burke.'

That confirmed it for me. He was talking about the man I had already met. I listened to Bill telling the story, without saying that I knew it. Jamie Burke wasn't a client, but he'd told me things in confidence and I owed him respect, and discretion . . .

CHAPTER SEVEN

Loftus, Cleveland
A few days earlier

Jamie Burke lived in High Row, Loftus, in one of the thirty-odd little terraced houses built in the nineteenth century to house the families of workers at the nearby Skinningrove ironstone mine. The houses are no longer home to mining families, and haven't been for the many decades since the mine closed, but a few descendants of the original occupants still live there. Jamie Burke was one of them, although he said he had never been in any sort of mine, let alone worked in one.

Jamie was a friend of Henry Bolckow, himself a friend and collaborator of mine. Although freelance, Henry was effectively my research department and IT consultant, and I owed him a lot. He was worried about Jamie, and had asked me to see if I could help him.

That rather took me aback, the idea that Henry had the time and energy to be worried about someone else, given how his own rackety life was lived on such a precarious edge. But I told him I would see what I could do.

It seemed unlikely that I could help, and I had a lot going on in my own life, but Henry had helped me often enough and I wasn't going to turn him down.

'I don't suppose there'll be any money in it, will there?' I joked.

'For you?' Henry queried, sounding aghast at such a sordid idea.

'For me, yes. I am supposed to be running a business here,' I pointed out, tongue in cheek.

What I didn't do was point out how often the shoe was on the other foot, with Henry looking for money-making jobs from me.

'I wouldn't have thought so,' he said stiffly. 'But Jamie isn't skint, if that's what you mean. He's made a bit of money over the years. It's just that it hasn't given him . . .'

He dried up, not sure how to put what he wanted to say.

'Security and peace of mind, perhaps?' I suggested helpfully, still smiling fondly at how Henry was struggling to cope with my enquiry.

'Yes, that's it,' he said. 'Peace and security.'

'OK. I'll see what I can do, Henry.'

***

Jamie's cottage was, as an estate agent might have put it, nicely situated. It was on a hill half a mile from the centre of the small town of Loftus, with a view of open fields at both back and front. Also at the front, in the distance, you could glimpse the Skinningrove steelworks and the associated industrial village of Carlin How. To your right was Huntcliff, where the moors meet the North Sea. The village of Skinningrove was out of sight, nestled in the valley of the Kilton Beck, below Carlin How.

It was a view that was very open, and a fascinating mix of old and new, industrial and rural. Full of interest, in other words. I could believe it might have helped to pull someone in difficulty back home.

Henry had given me the name of Jamie's street, but he hadn't known what the number of his house was. Seeing a young-ish woman washing the front windows of a house, I asked if she knew Jamie.

'Why?' she demanded. 'What do you want to know that for?'

A bit taken aback by the response, I turned away saying, 'Sorry I bothered you.'

'What do you want with him?' she insisted.

Turning back to face her, I said, 'It's a business matter. I need to talk to him. But I don't know the number of his house.'

She considered what I'd told her, sweeping her long blonde hair aside as she did so.

'I'm Frank Doy,' I added, deciding to present my credentials. 'I live at Risky Point, just along the coast. A mutual friend asked me to visit Jamie to see how he is.'

'Frank Doy? I've heard of you,' she said, nodding. 'You live by Jimmy Mack, don't you?'

'Yes. I live next door to him.'

'That's all right, then.'

Good old Jimmy! Not for the first time, I'd learned the advantage of living next to a local celebrity.

'You can't be too careful these days,' the woman added, making me wonder if they had a lot of burglaries.

'Jamie lives in this one,' she said, pointing. 'Next to me.'

'Thank you.'

I didn't bother asking if Jamie was in at present. I'd already had enough of a grilling.

CHAPTER EIGHT

'Jamie Burke?' I said to the man who opened the front door of the cottage.

He nodded.

'Frank Doy. I believe Henry Bolckow spoke to you about me?'

'Oh, yes! Pleased to meet you. Come on in.'

He stood aside and ushered me inside. I didn't need to look around or have the layout explained to me. It was the standard Cleveland miner's cottage, with a few standard twentieth-century add-ons. Originally two rooms up and two down, this one, like most of the others, now had an extension that housed a kitchen downstairs and a bathroom upstairs. The two original ground-floor rooms had been knocked into one big living room.

'Nice,' I said, glancing around as I sat down on a comfortable chair.

It was, too. Big windows at the front and back of the house meant it was light and bright. And the furniture looked modern and pretty new, as did the paintwork and wallpaper.

'This where you grew up?'

'No, but my grandparents had one just like it, further along the row. This one was pretty much derelict when I bought it, but doing it up has given me something to do with my time.'

'Oh? You're a skilled man, then. It doesn't look like a DIY job.'

'Well . . .'

He just shrugged, modestly.

'Henry is a good pal of mine,' I said, deciding it was time to move on to the main agenda. 'He's also a business associate who does a lot of work for and with me.'

'Work?' Jamie said with a smile. 'Henry? Doing what?'

'I don't know how much he told you about me, but I'm a freelance PI-cum-security consultant. Henry is my go-to IT specialist, who I also use for research. He's very good at it, and I would struggle without him.'

'Old Henry, eh? I wondered what he did for a living.'

'He told me you have a problem, and asked me to see if I can help in any way.'

He gave a rueful smile. 'I have a problem, all right. But I don't think it's one you can help with. Or anyone else, for that matter. I did tell Henry that.'

'Try me.'

He gathered his thoughts together, looking for a good place to start. My impression already was that he was a lonely man, glad to have the opportunity to talk about his situation, even if he did believe it would make no difference.

'Did Henry tell you I quit Witness Protection?'

I nodded.

'Six or seven months of that was long enough, more than enough.'

'Where were you?'

'A little village in Lincolnshire that was so insignificant, and so far out of the way, that if you ever went out of it, you'd be lucky to find your way back again.'

'Rural, then?'

'Yeah. Absolutely. There was nothing there but a few houses for farm workers. It was even worse for the local farmers. Their houses weren't even in the village.'

21

'So you just watched the grass grow?'

He nodded, and then sighed and looked as if he was wondering how he'd managed to stick it all that time.

What I wanted to hear was more about why he'd gone into the programme in the first place, but it seemed best to let him tell it in his own way.

'The isolation, in itself, wasn't the reason I left,' he said next.

'Oh?'

'A neighbour let me know two men had been looking for me when I was out one morning. That shouldn't have happened. People looking for me, I mean. Nobody was supposed to know where I was.'

'So you left?'

'That same day.'

Probably a wise move, I couldn't help thinking. The people responsible for his protection wouldn't have needed to look for him, and they certainly wouldn't have spoken to the neighbours about him. Obviously, he'd been found.

'You thought there'd been a leak?'

He nodded. 'I might have been wrong about that, but better to be wrong and alive than right and dead. I didn't wait to find out.'

'Tough decision, though.'

He shrugged. 'I'd had enough of Lincolnshire anyway. I wanted my life back. So here I am,' he added ruefully.

'Did you tell your handler, controller or whatever, what you were doing?'

He shook his head. 'All that went in the bin — Witness Protection, the new identity, everything. I reckoned I was better off on my own, looking after myself in a place I knew and understood. If my whereabouts had leaked once, it could happen again.'

There was a lot of sense in what he said. I'm sure the people responsible for running the Witness Protection system are honourable and conscientious, and take all the care they possibly can of their charges, but I also know that leaks from the system happen from time to time, either by accident or via bribery. The information lost or sold might well be trivial in itself, but in the hands of diligent investigators, it can be enough to put them on the right track.

'So you came back here?'

'Yes, back home. I'd had the house for a few years. I'd been doing it up.'

'I think it was a good move,' I told him. 'I would have done the same thing myself.'

'You would?'

'Definitely.'

Left Witness Protection, that is. What I didn't tell him was that coming back home might not have been such a great idea.

'Why did you need to go into protection in the first place, Jamie? Henry told me nothing about that.'

'It's a long story,' he said with a sigh. 'How long have you got?'

'As long as it takes.'

CHAPTER NINE

Jamie was a decent-looking, and decent-seeming, guy in his late thirties, I guessed. Short, dark hair. Medium height. Fit and strong-looking. Dressed in blue denim jeans and black tee shirt. His face didn't reveal a lot of emotion. A serious, rather worried look seemed its default expression, which wasn't surprising. He appeared to be pretty much an average, decent sort of guy. That was my take so far.

'What you have to understand,' he said wearily with a wry smile, 'is that I'm a wanted man.'

'I gathered that.'

'I identified, and am prepared to give evidence against, two men I saw murder three others.'

I couldn't help thinking he was right to be worried.

'We're talking about members of an organised crime gang, are we?'

He nodded. 'Pretty much, although it took time for me to realise it.'

'And you were part of it?'

Cue for a pause, accompanied by a weary sigh.

'I suppose I was,' he said ruefully. 'I can't deny it. I'm just naive, I suppose.

'One of the men who did the shooting was my boss, a businessman who owns an offshore engineering company, as well as plenty of other things. I was sort of aware of some dodgy stuff going on, but until the shooting happened, I wasn't involved in anything that seemed illegal.'

'What was the company you were working for?'

'KOSC — Kravertz Offshore Construction. They're based in Haverton Hill. Been going a few years now. Mostly concerned with decommissioning and dismantling oil rigs. To that extent, they're a legitimate business. I just didn't know about all the other stuff for a long time.'

'How come you were working for them?'

'I got sucked into it, a bit at a time. The dubious and illegal activities weren't obvious at first. Then, when I realised some of what was happening, it wasn't easy to leave, not if you wanted to stay alive and in one piece. The boss and his main sidekick are homicidal maniacs,' he added bitterly.

'So the state — prosecution, police or whoever — offered you a deal? Testify against them, or go down with them? Is that it?'

'Yes.' He looked at me defiantly. 'You going to judge me, as well?'

I shook my head. 'Not my job.'

I didn't like the picture that was emerging, but I needed more facts. So far, though, he wasn't looking like an innocent bystander.

CHAPTER TEN

Both Bill and I watched the flames dancing in the stove, me with a beer, Bill with another whisky. I reflected how my relationship with Bill can get a bit rocky at times. There have always been things he would be interested in, as a serving police officer, that I can't and don't tell him. And vice versa, of course. On the whole, that protects us both, and I believe Bill knows it as well as I do. That doesn't stop him sometimes trying to find out more than I want to tell him. And me keeping quiet.

The reality is that on occasion I have a client whose existence and activities I must treat with confidence, even if the police do have an interest. Then a bit of discretion serves both Bill and I well, and allows us to remain friends.

So far as Jamie Burke was concerned, I didn't have a particularly good reason to withhold my knowledge of the man, or the fact that we had met. As I said, Jamie wasn't a client. Even so, instinct told me it would be best to be guarded until I had worked out how everyone, and everything, stood with regard to him.

'Witness Protection,' I suggested, to keep the conversation going, 'doesn't always manage to protect the individual. And money can be involved, sometimes big money.'

Bill nodded agreement. 'That's probably what happened in this case. Somehow Burke's location and new identity were discovered. So he ran. And he did the worst thing he could have done. He came back home.'

'To hide in full sight, as it were.'

'That's about it,' Bill admitted with a sigh. 'But he's in the first place anyone looking seriously for him would visit. We found him within hours of him leaving Lincolnshire, which was where he'd been living.'

My unspoken thought, a worrying one, was that if Cleveland Police could find Jamie as easily as that, then so could people who had a more pressing reason to find and eliminate him.

'What do you know about his background?' I asked.

'He's a key witness in a murder case, which itself is part of a bigger ongoing investigation. He reckons he saw three men killed in cold blood by his boss and another man, and he's prepared to stand up in court and say so.'

'Who did he work for?'

'A guy who owns some sort of offshore business. KOSC. Kravertz Offshore Construction. Daniel Kravertz, who runs it, does various other things as well, some of them even legal. But he's a wrong 'un, as we used to say in the trade before that became a disciplinary offence. He's up to his eyes in all sorts of dodgy stuff. There's a big investigation going on into KOSC at the moment that involves the National Crime Agency, MI5, MI6, the Treasury, Customs and Exercise . . .'

'And Uncle Tom Cobley and all?'

'Exactly. We don't even know if Kravertz is the legal owner of the company. What we do know, is that he's a right bastard!'

'A crime boss, then?'

'That's as good a term for him as any. A nasty piece of work. You don't know him, do you?' he asked, looking at me speculatively.

I shook my head. 'I haven't had the pleasure. I have heard of KOSC, though. Don't they dismantle oil rigs, that sort of thing?'

'"That sort of thing" is right. They've got a base on the north side of the Tees, in Haverton Hill, where there used to be a shipyard before the industry went down the tubes.'

Bill went on to fill in a few more holes in the fabric of Jamie's story, giving me a better idea of how his problems had arisen. The lad seemed to have been sucked into events he had no control over. Then he'd had the guts to call a halt and get out. But look where that had got him!

'Are they getting anywhere with this investigation you mentioned?'

'It's been going on a year or two now, and I'm told they've pencilled in dates for laying charges and a first court appearance. It's likely to go on for a few more years yet, though. That's always the case when the people you're after have the wealth to retain an army of top-class lawyers, and Kravertz certainly seems to be in that category.'

The investigation, of course, could probably go on, and on, possibly forever. A court case wouldn't be the end of it either, even if a prosecution was successful. There would be an appeal if a guilty verdict was delivered. More than one. After the Appeal Court and the Supreme Court, the European Court of Justice or whatever it's called, would be on the case.

Meanwhile, a key witness like Jamie Burke would be left swinging in the wind, living in fear, possibly for the rest of his life.

'What have the police actually been doing to protect him?' I asked.

'Not a lot,' Bill said with a sigh. 'We don't have the manpower. Besides, he chose to leave Witness Protection himself — even if he did think he had good reason.'

'Well, good luck with it,' I said.

'Is that the best you can offer me?'

'I suppose we could take him fishing with us. Would that help?'

'Not much,' Bill said with another sigh. 'In fact, I can't see anything that would.'

28

On that pragmatic note, we changed the subject and got back to the idea of us getting the boat out again and going fishing ourselves.

Needless to say, Bill had made such inroads into Jimmy Mack's whisky by the end of the evening that he ended up staying the night.

Providing him with hospitality, and thereby keeping him off public roads, could be said to amount to me being a good citizen. Even so, Bill might still have been inclined to arrest me on some trumped-up charge had he known that, without telling him, I had already met and talked to Jamie Burke. I wouldn't put it past him.

CHAPTER ELEVEN

Haverton Hill, Teesside
Earlier that year

'Daniel, we love you like a brother. You know that. Otherwise, we wouldn't ask you to do this difficult task that we've been asked to take responsibility for, would we? You know that, don't you?'

'Sure. I know that,' Kravertz said with a scowl, thankful this was a phone conversation, not a video call.

'So we understand each other?'

'Sure we do.'

And sure he did. There was no way he could say no to these people. They owned him. That was the truth of it. He didn't like the idea, but it was true. Everything he had, and had achieved, was down to them. There would be no KOSC without them.

'Are we good, Daniel?'

'We're good. You don't need to worry about that.'

'By December sixteenth, remember. You've got plenty of time, many months, but everything must be ready by then. Ready for the Christmas party!'

* * *

Afterwards, Kravertz ran through a couple of things in his mind, sorting out where this left him. His hope was that one day he would be invited to join the inner circle, and talk to others as Manny had spoken to him. One day. Not yet, though. He had some way to go before he got to that position.

The reality was that he had to be patient and continue to display his loyalty and usefulness to the organisation — the Brotherhood, as Manny called it. Otherwise, he would never reach the inner circle. Nor would he retain the power and wealth that being the owner of KOSC gave him.

Owner? He gave a wry smile at his image in the bathroom mirror. Ostensibly, he was the owner of the company, but that was only achieved with the money made available to him by the organisation. Upset or deny Manny, and that loan could be rescinded, and his being unable to repay the loan would be unacceptable. The consequences that would then follow were not in doubt, which meant that failure to deliver what the organisation wanted of him was unthinkable.

So he had better get going and find the divers he would need. He had quite a few months to get the job done, but he figured he was going to need them all.

CHAPTER TWELVE

Kravertz knew exactly what he had to do, and he had got on with it. The first set of divers were up for it, especially when he told them how much he was prepared to pay them. The explosives were taken out to them in their support ship, along with all the usual equipment, and a few extras they needed for the job.

The work took a few weeks, but it got done — almost.

For the final task, the placing of the master switch along with the last package of explosives, he had decided to use a different dive team, to avoid any of them knowing the full picture. It was a mistake. And that was when he ran into problems. He chose the wrong team. They refused to do it.

Then all hell was let loose!

He and his main man, Jed Smith, knew what had to be done. They had previously spoken of this possibility, but only theoretically, as in an unlikely situation. Now the unlikely situation had arisen and there was no way the dive team could be allowed to walk out of the picture knowing what they knew. Decisive action had to be taken, and it was.

Then another error of judgement on Kravertz's part came home to roost. They had brought Burke along for the experience — to blood him, as it were, and move him to another stage in his apprenticeship. But it was the wrong time and the wrong place. Burke had made his feelings clear and run out on them. They were unable to stop him, and hadn't been able to catch up with him ever since.

Months had been spent hunting Burke, without success. They had finally got close to him in Lincolnshire, thanks to inside information, but not close enough. He had run again.

It was only now, when they were so close to the end of the project that they had been given another opportunity, one they couldn't afford to waste. It seemed he had come back home. Why that was remained unclear, but it didn't matter at all. What Kravertz knew was that he had been handed a lifeline, a reprieve, one he couldn't afford to miss out on.

Meanwhile, the official investigation into him and his company trundled on, but he was untroubled by that. It hadn't stopped him finding another dive team and completing the preparatory work needed to get the job done. The way he looked at it was that the investigators couldn't have much on him, or he would have been arrested by now. Take out Burke, and they would have next to nothing at all.

So long as the lawyers could hold off arrest, charge and prosecution, he was OK. He could live with how things were. Only when the investigators believed they had a case that would stand up in court would he be seriously worried. Then he would simply vanish. His preparations to do so had long been in place. Until then, if it ever happened, he would continue doing what he did, and only quit and disappear when it suited him.

But the key to all this was Burke. Take him out, and a vanishing act would be unnecessary. He would be safe.

CHAPTER THIRTEEN

Risky Point

The day after my fireside drinks with part of the Cleveland Constabulary, I was outside the cottage blowing up a tyre on the Land Rover when I heard someone call to me. It was him, Jamie Burke, heading my way on foot. I straightened up and turned towards him, wondering if something had happened.

'So this is where you live, Frank?' he said with a smile.

'Morning, Jamie! How are you doing?'

'Fine, thanks. I'm just out for a walk, and thought I would come this way for a change.'

He stopped and turned round to look at my cottage, Jimmy Mack's cottage and then the cliff edge. I could see what he was thinking, but he didn't say it. I said it for him.

'We're on borrowed time, here, Jamie. Jimmy Mack, my neighbour, will tell you that. But we like it. So we stay anyway.'

He laughed. 'It doesn't worry you?'

'You get used to it. One day the cliff will erode some more, no doubt, but for now we're in a great position.'

'Wonderful view,' he said, nodding. 'I wouldn't want to leave here either.'

I didn't tell him he was living more dangerously than me. He didn't need reminding.

'Fancy a coffee, Jamie? I was just going inside to put the kettle on, now I've finished blowing this thing back up.'

I gave the tyre a kick that expressed my frustration with it.

'A fine old Landy, eh?' he said, eyeing my favourite vehicle. 'You can't beat 'em.'

'You'll have had plenty of experience of them in the army, I suppose?'

'Some. They never let you down, and if anything does go wrong you can usually fix it yourself. No computers in 'em. So you don't need IT boffins and a state-of-the-art garage.'

'You're right there. And you wouldn't believe what this one has had to put up with from me.'

'So it might deserve a new tyre?'

'Still plenty of miles in this one. It just keeps losing pressure.'

'The tread looks OK. I can see that. Maybe rust on the wheel rim is stopping it sealing properly?'

'You could be right. I'll have to get it seen to.'

'You want me to take a look at it for you? Plenty of time on my hands.'

'I'll take you up on that, Jamie! Now let's go for that hot drink.'

I wasn't sure I was doing the right thing, accepting his offer. Not surprisingly, he gave the impression he was lonely, and he seemed a bit too eager to make a new friend. I didn't want to become his new best buddy and first port of call. I had enough on my plate.

On the other hand, I was getting tired of blowing the damned tyre up. It had become almost a daily requirement. So why not let him have at it?

Over coffee, I asked him if anything had happened since I saw him.

'No.' He shook his head and added, 'I almost wish it would. Just sitting about waiting, and expecting, gets on your nerves.'

I nodded. I could understand that.

'Perhaps getting a job of some kind would be better for you?'

'Yeah. It's a pity I've got all the DIY on the house done. That's kept me busy, and it took my mind off things a bit. I've been looking around for a job, but I haven't seen anything I fancy yet.'

My view was that almost any kind of job would help. He just needed something to do, something to get him out more.

'Are you worried about the house, Jamie?'

'When I'm out, you mean?' He shook his head. 'No. Jenny, a neighbour, keeps an eye on things when I'm not there.'

'Would that be the woman I met the other day, when I was looking for you?'

'Probably.'

'She gave me a pretty ferocious grilling before she would tell me where you lived. I had to tell her I lived here, next to Jimmy Mack, before she decided I was acceptable and relented.'

He chuckled. 'She's a good lass, Jenny. And she's always around. She has a youngster, and she's on her own with him. So she's home most of the time, which is good for me. We get on well together.'

I smiled, recalling how getting past her had been like running the gauntlet.

'I'd like you to let Henry know I'm all right, if you would, Frank. I don't want him worrying about me, and he won't be reassured if I tell him myself. Could you have a word with him?'

So that was what the visit was about. I'd thought there must be something behind it. I was quite touched. Despite his own situation, Jamie was concerned his old friend would be worrying about him.

'I'll tell him,' I said with a smile. 'I know what you mean. Henry has enough to be worried about, given his lifestyle.'

* * *

When Jamie decided he'd better be going, I said I would accompany him. I needed a walk myself, and the clifftop route back towards Loftus via Boulby is a route with magnificent views that always stirs the spirits. The cliffs are impressive. At their peak, they're supposed to be six-hundred feet from foreshore to summit, which makes them the highest in England.

I soon found that walking with Jamie wasn't a leisurely experience. That suited me, actually. I needed the exercise. But I was surprised. I was even more surprised when he decided to drop down from the path to get a better view of some old alum workings. It wasn't easy going, and I didn't feel the need to share the experience. I waited for him to return. It didn't take him long, and I was impressed by his speed coming uphill over extremely rough and uncertain ground.

'You're keeping yourself pretty fit, Jamie,' I remarked as we resumed our walk.

He chuckled at that. 'Not as fit as I used to be,' he said.

'Even so. Do you do much these days?'

'Not in the way of exercise, if that's what you mean. But I'm pretty active. I don't sit around the house all day.'

'Running and skipping, perhaps?' I asked, dredging my memory for what I knew of a boxer's training regime, which wasn't much.

'Some of that, when I feel like it. I've also rigged up a heavy bag and a fast-ball in the backyard. Banging away at them works up a sweat. Mostly, though, I just walk. I spend far more time doing that than anything else.'

'Walking, huh? At last, Jamie, you've mentioned something I'm capable of doing.'

CHAPTER FOURTEEN

It was a couple of days later that I got a phone call I hadn't expected, but which was very welcome.

'Frank, I owe you an apology. What happened shouldn't have happened, and I am truly sorry that it did.'

'That's very gracious of you, Leon,' I said, with a smile and a feeling of relief.

'You were very angry, I think?'

'And very worried! I don't mind admitting it.'

'I understand. I say again, it should not have happened. Frank, we have been friends a long time. I would like our friendship to continue.'

'Me, too.'

'How can I make amends?'

'Nothing needs doing, Leon. We are friends. And what happened was . . . an accident. Nothing more, and not your fault.'

'I am happy to hear you say that.'

'Good. How are things with you, Leon? What on earth were you doing the other day in my sea? And what about that trawler — surely it's not yours?'

'The trawler is ours, yes. We are doing some work in the North Sea for the British Admiralty. Other government departments are also involved. I am not sure which ones. But the Admiralty is the main one. The two gentlemen with me on the bridge when you arrived were from the Admiralty.'

'That sounds interesting. A new business venture for you, eh? I'd been wondering if you were impacted by the fallout from what's been happening in Ukraine.'

'The sanctions, you mean? Oh, no! I may be part of the Russian diaspora, but I am a good guy in the eyes of the West. So we are no more affected than most businesses. Your own government seems to like me, and sometimes asks me to do work for them. One reason is that I give them a channel into Russia, where I have many contacts, of course.

'Besides, we Podolskys are all Czech citizens now, and citizens of the European Union. You don't need to worry about us.'

'I'm relieved to hear it, Leon, not that I ever really thought there would be a problem.'

The reality was that the Podolskys, and their business operations, were based in the Czech Republic because it was much safer for them to be there than in their homeland. In fact, almost anywhere outside Russia was safer for them. They were no friends of the Kremlin, despite their origins.

'Frank, I meant what I said when I told you there is a job, a very urgent job actually, that I would like you to consider. I will not speak of it on the phone, but I believe it would interest you very much. Can I ask you to reconsider and hear me out?'

It took me no more than a moment to reconsider and then say yes, of course I was interested.

The truth was that I was weary and a bit flat after a particularly busy time for me lately. Life at Risky Point isn't always a gentle stroll, contrary to what Bill Peart sometimes suggests. I felt in need not of a rest, but of a change of scene. I needed to get away, and go to . . . well, almost anywhere that wasn't here. That was why Leon Podolsky's bait lured me.

'What's the job?'

'Not over the phone, Frank. Come and see me in Prague.'

'You're back there, are you?'

'For the moment.'

'Can you at least tell me something in general terms? I need to have some idea what to expect.'

After a brief hesitation, he said, 'Safeguarding my sister. It's short term, and urgent.'

'Which sister?'

'The one that doesn't like flying.'

Olga, in other words.

That was enough for me.

'See you in Prague,' I told him.

CHAPTER FIFTEEN

Haverton Hill

'Well, Daniel, you've got a big problem now, haven't you?'

Kravertz nodded.

Manny couldn't see him do it. So Kravertz spoke, as well, and said he did. He admitted he had a problem.

'You doing something about it?'

'Yeah. We're right on him. Burke's going nowhere.'

'I need to tell you something, Daniel. The way we see it, it's your problem — not ours. And we expect you to fix it. You clear about that?'

'Sure, Manny. Don't worry about it. I'll get it fixed.'

'Good. Now let me tell you about the problem we both have, our joint problem.'

'Right.'

'There are people who suspect something is going on, and they're investigating to see if anything has been interfered with. I'm talking about the Brits' Admiralty. They've brought in the Podolsky family to help with the investigation.'

'Who are they?'

'Ethnic Russians, but domiciled in the Czech Republic. They may even be Czechs now, and EU citizens.'

'Never heard of them. What do they do?'

'Many things, Daniel. They have an extensive business empire. Right now, there is only one thing they do that is of interest to us. They're good at monitoring subsea infrastructure — pipelines and such.'

'Ah!'

Kravertz rolled his eyes skywards. *So Manny thinks I don't know what subsea stuff means? Me, in this business for the past ten years?*

'Yeah. We're told they've had a lot of experience of this kind of work in the Persian Gulf and the Red Sea. A lot of success, too, in stopping sabotage missions there.'

Kravertz could now see where this was heading, or he thought he could.

'So we need to watch out for them? Is that what you're telling me, Manny?'

'More than that, Daniel. The key player is one of the sisters of Leon Podolsky, the guy who runs the business. She's some sort of genius with IT and has to be stopped from interfering — permanently! Stop her, and the Podolskys are finished. Not just with this investigation, either. Maybe altogether.'

Kravertz wasn't so sure now that he knew what was coming. He kept quiet, and waited.

'So we want you to visit the Czech Republic, Daniel — in person — and see that she's taken out. Eliminate her,' Manny added, in case his meaning wasn't clear.

'You'll be met by Czechs who cooperate with us. Zeman is the main guy there. He'll look after you and show you around. He might even have paved the way for you already. So go there, and get it done — if Zeman hasn't already managed to do it.'

Frowning, Kravertz nodded and listened. He didn't like it, but he had no choice, not when Manny was telling him how it had to be.

'Daniel, forget about Burke for now. Concentrate on neutralising Olga Podolsky. That's your top priority.'

CHAPTER SIXTEEN

After Leon's call, I wondered what was happening. What was the reason for Leon's increased concern about Olga? Why the urgency? Why now?

I knew Olga, and liked her a lot. I would be very happy to work as her close protection officer, as it's called in the trade. For a short while, anyway. And Leon paid good money.

So what was wrong with the invitation and job offer? Nothing at all. Not unless you knew Leon and the kind of trouble the Podolskys attracted, which I did. Then you had to think twice, which I also did.

Then I thought to hell with it, and just went anyway.

* * *

I'd worked in Prague for Leon a couple of times, and I liked the place. It's a big, historic city, the capital of the Czech Republic — or Czechia, as some would have us call it now. Once upon a time, though, it was home to the kings of Bohemia, and far beyond, the cosmopolitan centre of the Holy Roman Empire. The buildings, the bridges over the Vltava River, Old Town Square, and the Little Quarter all reflect that history, and then some. The beer, a pilsener, is pretty good too.

As usual with Leon, urgent meant urgent. He wanted me to get myself there as soon as possible, whatever time of day or night it was when I arrived. Even if I hadn't been able to tell him in advance about my flight, he assured me, I would be collected immediately from the airport.

I had to smile at that. It meant he had someone monitoring the airline passenger lists. Typical of Leon. Nothing, no detail, overlooked. That was how he ran his whole business empire.

Furthermore, he insisted, I was not, on any account, to take a taxi or use either the very good bus service or the excellent Metro system to travel into the city centre. Transportation would be provided.

A bit over the top? Well, a less cynical person than myself might have thought it was all a bit odd. I just nodded and thought there must be an enhanced security issue, which was something else that wasn't unusual where Leon was concerned.

I knew of old that he had very good reason to be ultra careful about both his own safety and that of everyone else within his orbit. Family, friends, staff — everyone! He had more than his share of opponents and enemies, and he lived his life on a very precipitous edge, financially and politically, as well as security wise. Being a wealthy businessman of Russian extraction, an oligarch if you like, had serious drawbacks, regardless of whether you lived in Moscow, London or anywhere else. Even Prague, for that matter.

* * *

I flew from Newcastle early the next morning, November twelfth, to be precise. A familiar face met me at Vaclav Havel Airport Prague, just on the edge of the city. Impeccably polite, stern, strong, unflappable, Charles was . . . what, exactly? Well, I'd never been entirely sure what he, or his job title, was. Manager of Leon's hotel in Vysehrad; General Factotum; Security Chief; ruthless assassin when needed to be . . . To my knowledge, you could call him any or all of those things, and probably more.

Above all, though, I knew him as a good man and someone unfailingly loyal to the Podolsky family. Leon couldn't have functioned without people like Charles around him.

I caught Charles's eye amid the press of meeters and greeters with posh name boards and handwritten cards awaiting new arrivals. With only the slightest motion of his head, he acknowledged me and invited me to follow him. There was no welcome ceremony at all. Not even the faintest of smiles. As ever, concern for security overrode all other considerations.

I nodded and duly followed as he strode purposefully out of the terminal building and headed towards a short-stay parking area nearby. As we made our way, my own internal security antennae were activated, and soon they were bristling. I glanced sideways and my step faltered as I noticed a man on each side, but a couple of car widths away, keeping pace with us.

'They are with us, Mr Doy,' Charles said quietly over his shoulder, picking up on my hesitation without looking round.

'Good to know!' I replied with a smile of relief that he couldn't possibly see, but might well have known about anyway.

It was so familiar. All this, all these precautions, went with the territory. Leon's world. It matched my remembered experience of Prague. This was life as Leon knew and lived it: the constant need for vigilance, and to anticipate and be prepared to respond to threat without notice. It was the up-and-down life of an expat Russian businessman and political activist who had seldom, and then only briefly, ceased to be targeted by the Kremlin.

It was why Leon, like the Russian president himself, kept his immediate family distant and safe in Switzerland, perhaps the one country in the world permanently observing a truce between warring adversaries, if they could afford to live there.

Well, some of Leon's family, at least. His wife and children. His two sisters were right here in Prague with him, Lenka a ferocious fighting woman and pilot, and Olga a dreamy IT genius. There might well have been other family members, too, but they were the only ones I knew about. Leon guarded his family more closely than a miser his gold.

45

Our little procession reached a Mercedes SUV. Both the driver and a front-seat passenger had seen us coming and got out of the vehicle to meet us. Charles ushered me into the back seat and climbed in beside me. The protection team, the men walking either side of us, got into other vehicles.

Charles issued a quick burst of rapid Czech to our driver, who along with the passenger had resumed his seat. Then we were off, moving briskly towards the exit.

Now we were safely in transit, Charles turned to me with a smile. 'Welcome back to Prague, Mr Doy! It is very good to see you.'

'Thank you, Charles. It's good to see you, too.'

'I must apologise for the precautions we took at the airport. They did not make for a pleasant arrival, but perhaps you will recall how it is here for us. They were necessary, I assure you, even more so than usual.'

'Charles, believe me, I am very happy with anything done to protect me. I remember how dangerous life can be at times in this city.'

'Good. The journey will take us approximately twenty minutes. If you will excuse me, I must give the drivers more instructions now.'

So both men in the front seats were drivers, eh? Having two of them meant there was cover in the event of one of them being taken out or rendered inactive for any reason. It was another illustration of Leon's clear thinking and readiness to meet risk. Leave as little as possible to chance.

All the same, it made me wonder again what I was getting into this time. In one sense, of course, I knew. Working for Leon was always the same. Every time. Uncertain and dangerous. Perversely, perhaps, that was one reason why I was here again. There was never time for boredom or feeling out of sorts when you were in Leon's world.

I nodded to Charles to indicate I appreciated that he had business to discuss with the drivers. Then I turned my head to gaze out of the window at the passing scene.

It was just as well that I did.

CHAPTER SEVENTEEN

A van had come from a side road and was heading straight for us at speed. We were broadside onto it, and I looked like being at the point of impact. I yelled a warning and hurled myself sideways, sprawling over Charles.

Our driver had no time to react. The van hit us with an almighty crash. The car rocked, threatened to turn over and swivelled round, locked to the van. My head slammed into something hard. My ears shuddered with the agonising screech of tearing metal. The air was full of fragments of shattered window glass. Everything was a blur.

All movement stopped. And then automatic gunfire started up somewhere close by. I was shocked, dazed and in pain, but the momentary warning I'd had of the impending crash had given me a chance of survival. I knew I had to get out — fast!

I wasn't stunned. I could move. Charles hadn't been so lucky. He was out of it. I scrambled over him, opened the door on his side of the car and flopped out on to the ground. Then I reached back to pull him out after me.

He was conscious, I realised, but barely. I laid him on the ground. Stunned and struggling to breathe, it looked like he'd suffered head and chest injuries. Blood was leaking from some part of him.

More gunfire. Closer! My head jerked up and round, as I tried to locate where it was coming from. I had no idea. It was definitely gunfire, but that was all I was sure of. More than one gun, as well. A battle.

I couldn't see anything, and didn't know what was happening. The action was taking place somewhere on the far side of the car, and I wasn't going to stand up or stick my head round the corner to check it out.

There was a strong smell of petrol now, probably leaking from a ruptured tank.

A fireball could be erupting very soon. I couldn't stay here. I had to move. And move Charles as well. Our two drivers were inside the car still, giving no signs of life. I couldn't look for help from them.

Desperate, I glanced around, trying to spot a safer place. We were on the narrow median of a double carriageway, a dusty strip of desiccated grass. All the vehicles on the far side of the road that I could see had stopped, many having piled into each other. Horns were blaring. Alarms screeching. Stalled and crashed vehicles everywhere I looked.

They didn't really offer safety, but there was nothing else to get behind. I had to reach one of them. Charles seemed to be regaining his wits, but he was badly hurt. I would have to carry or drag him.

Pushing up on to my knees, I risked a quick glance into the front of the car. The drivers were there still, still unmoving. No help from them possible. The head of the one who had been a passenger lay on his shoulder, telling me he had a broken neck. The body of the man behind the steering wheel was still in place, but his head had gone.

The gunfire and the whizz of bullets in the air was much closer now. I guessed our protection squad in the other cars were engaged in a gun battle with the attackers. They couldn't help me any more than they were doing already. I swung back round to Charles, who was definitely conscious now.

'Charles, we have to move!'

'Yes,' he whispered drowsily.

'I want to get us behind one of the cars on the other side of the road, or that truck over there. OK?'

He grunted what might have been agreement.

'Good man!' I told him.

He probably shouldn't be moved. I knew that. But I wasn't staying here, and I couldn't just leave him and hope for the best. Moving him was the least bad option. If I left him, he probably wouldn't survive anyway. Our attackers were likely to make sure of that, even if his injuries didn't.

I hauled him off the ground and heaved him across my shoulders. Then I got into a crouch and set off in an ungainly, lurching stagger across two lanes of roadway to collapse and shelter behind the wheels of a big wagon on the far side. We joined the wagon driver, who must have decided his cab was not a good place to be.

I set Charles down as gently as I could, putting him in a seated position, his back against one of the truck's wheels. He inclined his head slightly in what I took as a nod to express his thanks, but he didn't speak. Throughout it all, despite the pain I was sure he was in, he hadn't uttered a squeak in protest. Tough man, Charles. But I'd long known that.

Straightening up and looking around, I could see other people sheltering in little groups behind vehicles. We were in good company, and perhaps in a slightly better position than we had been.

I still didn't know what was happening, though. All I really knew was that we had been attacked and a gun battle was raging, presumably between the attackers and our back-up team.

When I stuck my head out, I still couldn't see the people doing the shooting, or anybody at all moving. Mostly what I could see was long lines of stationary vehicles in every direction. This part of Prague had come to a stop.

I wondered if we could just wait here and sit it out until help came, but I knew there was little chance of that happening. It would take time for an armed emergency response team to get here, time for the people looking for us to finish the job.

Then there was movement. I saw three masked men approaching our abandoned car. One fired a submachine gun into the interior. It seemed pointless, given the condition of the two drivers. Flames immediately burst into life with a roar, which may have been what was intended.

I pulled back into cover when the men left the blaze and started searching the nearby area, looking for something, or someone. Looking for us, I was sure. Perhaps even just for me.

What to do? I glanced around, more desperate than ever, searching for something, anything, that might help.

Charles revived with a start and stared questioningly at me.

'They're still looking for us,' I told him. 'They know we can't be far away.'

There didn't seem much we could do about it either. No sign of the back-up crew. Dead now, probably, given that the gunfire had almost ceased. It looked like none of us was intended to survive.

'Take . . . this,' Charles whispered, thrusting something into my belly.

I looked down. It was a gun, a Glock pistol.

'It's no use to me,' he croaked.

'Are you sure?'

He gave a nod. Then he rallied and said in a weak voice, 'I am sorry. We have failed you.'

'Oh, no!' I assured him more confidently than I felt. 'We're not done yet.'

I took the gun. It was a familiar model. I even had one just like it hidden away at home. It wouldn't be much competition for a man with a submachine gun, but it was better than nothing.

'I will go,' Charles said. 'They don't know you. But they know me.'

I was looking the other way, and, before I realised what he meant, he had somehow struggled to his feet and embarked on a stumbling, lurching run out into the open, heading down the road between the stranded vehicles.

50

CHAPTER EIGHTEEN

I grimaced. *How the hell . . . ?*

Charles had taken me completely by surprise. His move had happened so fast I'd had no chance of stopping him. It was hard even to believe he'd been capable of it.

He got ten or fifteen yards before there was a fusillade of gunshots and he went down in a twitching heap.

A man with a submachine gun appeared. For the moment, he had eyes only for the body on the ground in front of him. But it would be my turn next. He knew now where we'd been sheltering.

As he turned towards my position, I raised the Glock and started shooting. I didn't bother about aiming the gun. I was so desperate, I just hoped and fired.

He seemed to be hit once or twice. At least, he staggered. But I didn't really know. Not until his body arced, his arms flung wide. Then the gun fell out of his grasp as he slumped to the ground.

Two more men came to join him. I turned towards them, but saw they had no interest in continuing the action. They were both staggering, as if wounded themselves. They gave the man I had shot a cursory glance and turned to limp away, holding on to each other for support.

The truck driver started jabbering away at me. I shook my head and said, '*Promǐn. Nemluvím čeština.*' Sorry. I don't speak Czech.

He seemed to understand what I meant. Just as well. That was close to my limit in the language.

The gunfire had finished now. I wondered if the action was over. It had been a desperate few minutes.

I also wondered if it was the back-up crew that had shot the two wounded men I had just seen retreating. Probably. Someone had. Who else could it have been?

I left cover and ran to check on Charles. To my astonishment, he was alive still — barely. He was unconscious and covered in a lot more blood now, but I could feel a pulse in his neck. I dropped to my knees and started doing what I could to stem the bleeding.

It was pretty hopeless, a lost cause, it seemed. Realistically, his chances were abysmal, but I didn't allow myself to think that way. I just concentrated on doing what little I could.

'Mr Doy!' a voice somewhere behind me said. 'Let me help. You are hurt?'

I didn't look round, but I was relieved to hear a friendly sounding voice, and I shook my head. It had to be a survivor from the back-up team. So it wasn't just me left to cope with the situation, after all.

'I'm OK,' I panted. 'But this man is very badly hurt. Please phone for help — ambulance, doctor!'

The man came into view and squatted down beside me.

'Get help!' I yelled at him.

'Leon will be here soon,' he said calmly.

'Not Leon! We need doctors, ambulance . . .'

'Leon knows. I have told him.'

I redoubled my efforts on Charles. The new arrival's calmness was infuriating, but he seemed to know what he was doing. He began to help tear strips from Charles's shirt, to use as tourniquets and patches. Together, we staunched the worst of the blood flow. Then the man took off his jacket, folded it and placed it under Charles's head before we turned him on to his side, trying to keep his airways clear.

52

I had been aware for a minute or two of something approaching that was making a lot of noise. Now the noise was directly overhead, and very loud. I pulled back and looked up. A helicopter was descending. Press, police? I had no idea. I glanced at the man alongside me.

'Leon!' he shouted. 'He is here.'

CHAPTER NINETEEN

It was a very brisk, efficient operation, in typical Podolsky style. The noise and sheer force of the chopper cleared bystanders out of the way as it came down to land nearby on the median. The door at the side was already open, and even before wheels touched the ground, variously attired figures leapt out.

Those in white knew exactly where Charles was lying and what to do about it. In seconds they had him scooped up on to a stretcher and away into the chopper. Seeing Leon beckoning from the doorway, I followed. So did the back-up guy who had been helping me tend to Charles. It couldn't have been more than a minute or two before we were air-borne and rapidly lifting away from the ground.

Leon steered me into a seat and squeezed my arm in welcome before turning away to have a quick word with the back-up guy. Then he went to watch over the medics tending to Charles. I could see plasma bottles being held up and lots of other signs of emergency response. Battlefield medical practice going to work. Bad as his condition was, at least Charles was in good hands.

It was very noisy, of course, far too noisy, as it always is in a helicopter. I sat still and kept out of the way. This wasn't my time. There was no point in attempting conversation without wearing an earpiece and mic. Besides, I was sore and aching, battered and bruised, and my head was buzzing. I didn't need conversation. I needed to slow down, relax a bit and try to recover.

How long had it been since I'd screamed a warning as the van came at us? It was impossible to say. Minutes, not hours, and no more than a few. Everything had happened so damn fast, too fast for the brain to remember and make sense of. Men I had only just met, and barely seen, and others I hadn't even met or seen at all, had been killed in an inexplicable maelstrom of violence.

Then there was Charles, a man I liked and respected, who was hovering at death's door, if he hadn't already gone through it. And for what? Why?

When Leon had said he needed my help, he hadn't said what he needed it for. No mention had been made of fighting pitched battles on the streets of a European capital city. I should have known, of course, that he wasn't just tossing an old friend a fun party invitation, and the chance to earn a little extra money on the side. He wasn't like that. Leon was all business. I should have realised something serious was going on when he said he had an urgent job for me, or even when he'd had me hauled out to the trawler

And I should have weighed all that against my restless and no doubt temporary disaffection with life at Risky Point. Also, I should have recalled more fully where helping Leon out in the past had got me. It had never been a carefree, happy experience. The lifestyle that he and those around him led wasn't like that. Leon and friends, family as well, had always bounced from one crisis to another.

Of course, what had just happened to me was what poor old Jamie Burke had been living in fear of for a very long time. The only difference was that I had survived, whereas he might not when the day came for the shooting to start.

* * *

55

Leon never left Charles's side while the medics attended to him on the short flight before the chopper lowered itself on to the flat top of a fairly high modern building that I recognised. I had wondered where Charles would be taken, but I should have known it wouldn't be to an ordinary hospital. Instead, it was to the private medical centre that Leon owned, and that I had once visited. I knew it was staffed by the best medics that money, and Leon's magnetism, could attract. No doubt, there would be trauma specialists here, a category of medicine men probably often needed by the Podolskys.

Landing a helicopter on top of a high-rise city building surrounded by buildings of like size is a pretty difficult feat, it seemed to me, but the pilot managed it fast and without hesitation. Only a very few minutes after being brought on board, Charles was out of the aircraft again and headed for an elevator that would whisk him down to a superbly equipped emergency operating theatre. If he had even the slightest chance of survival, which I very much doubted, this was undoubtedly the very best place for him to be.

Typically, Leon stayed behind at the medical centre when the chopper took off again a minute or two later. I knew he would want to be with his man. Loyalty ran both ways in this organisation. He was to his people as they were to him. That went a long way to explain why, together, they were such an effective outfit.

I stayed where I was. Inevitably, I was a passenger in more than one sense now. I had no idea what would happen next, or where we would go. Even so, I didn't doubt that I was in good hands, too. The pilot, and the remaining member of the Podolsky staff still on board, would know exactly what to do and where to take me.

It was only when the chopper began its descent a few minutes later that I realised two things: the identity of the pilot, and where we were. The former was Leon's tough sister, Lenka; the latter was the grounds of his large villa in Střesovice, a wealthy old garden suburb to the west of Hradčany, where castle, cathedral and the seat of government of the Czech Republic are all located. I knew them both, Lenka and Střesovice.

CHAPTER TWENTY

After we landed, the member of staff escorted me from the helicopter and across the lawn to the handsome villa that dominated the property. Lenka had given me a wave from the cockpit, but there had been no chance to speak to her. Immediately after our exit, the chopper had lifted back into the sky, going I knew not where. The man with me just shrugged and smiled when I asked him. Either he didn't know, or I had asked for information that wild horses wouldn't drag out of him.

My guess was that Lenka was heading back to the medical centre, but I didn't think she would be bringing Leon home any time soon. To put it another way, if she did, the news would be bad. It would mean that Charles hadn't made it. Knowing Leon as I did, I didn't believe he would leave Charles's side until the question of his survival was resolved, one way or the other.

When we reached the villa, my guide handed me over to a bonny middle-aged woman. Then he smiled at me, bowed and withdrew.

'Good day, Mr Doy,' the woman said in perfect English, and with a welcoming smile of her own. 'My name is Věra. I am the housekeeper here. Mr Podolsky has asked me to welcome you and provide everything you require. He apologises

for not being here himself, but says he knows you will understand. It is a time of emergency.'

Indeed, I did understand.

* * *

Věra showed me to the room I was to use and asked if I
would like a meal. Not now, I said, thanking her for the offer.
But I would like a lot of coffee. She told me a flask would be
brought to my room.

I also had in mind that I would like a shower very much,
and a change of clothing. My room was en-suite. So I could
have the former, but my spare clothes, along with much else,
had gone up in flames back at the ambush site.

I had the shower and a cup of coffee before lying down
in a bathrobe to rest. After a while I got up, re-dressed and
wandered outside to take a look at my surroundings before
the day ended.

The other time I had been here had been a few weeks
later in the year, when everything had been deep in snow.
Now it was autumn still, a lovely November afternoon, and
the world was very colourful. The still-leafy deciduous trees
in the garden, mostly poplars and plane trees, were ablaze in
the late sunshine, and the garden generally was altogether
beautiful and peaceful. After my hectic arrival in the city
I needed a bit of that, beauty and peace, to help reset my
bearings.

Leon's house was set on a small rise. Not a hill, exactly,
but a gentle uplift in the landscape that gave a view of a great
swathe of the centre of the city. The view was dominated by
the castle and cathedral complex of Hradčany to the east.
A few degrees to the south, it was possible to make out the
valley of the Vltava, the river that bisects the city.

There were also television and communication towers
in sight, and modern high-rise buildings and historic church
spires dotted across the complex and ancient urban landscape.
To my eye, as I wandered between the old trees scattered

across Leon's garden, it was a fascinating scene, and it gave me a welcome shift of focus from the morning's events.

In time, I picked out a fast-moving bird coming from the city centre. It soon revealed itself to be a helicopter coming this way. Bringing Leon, perhaps? That brought me back to the day's reality with a jerk. I grimaced as I wondered what the news would be of Charles, as well as of everything else.

Thinking about my arrival at the airport, and the mayhem that followed, I also wondered what the fallout from all that would be. There would certainly be some, enough perhaps to make Leon think he shouldn't have invited me. For a start, he was a number of other good men down now, as well as Charles. Then, given his origins, I thought he might have a hard time telling the police about the attack, and maybe an even harder time explaining his use of a helicopter to remove survivors of the ambush from a major crime scene.

Then there was my own name. I wondered if that would come up, and hoped it wouldn't. If it did, I could foresee months, even years, of trying to avoid and resist Czech attempts to extradite me as a witness, if nothing else. I could do without that.

I pulled myself together. Both I and Leon's people meeting me, had been innocents, not instigators, of the morning's events. As for Leon and the evacuation, he'd done his very best to save a life, using his own resources. How could he be faulted for that? Leon was a good guy in all this.

He was also an operator, I reminded myself with a rueful smile. He would probably cope, as he always did. At least, I hoped so.

* * *

The helicopter came in and landed without fuss, reminding me yet again that Lenka, too, was a skilled and effective operator. In terms of action and getting practical things done in dangerous situations, there seemed to be no limit to her abilities. Although we had got off to a rocky start when we first met, we had subsequently worked well together and gained each other's respect. Saving each other's life along the way had had something to do with that, I reminded myself with a wry smile.

But only Leon emerged from the aircraft. He dropped to the ground and strode towards me, a smile lighting up his face.

'Frank!' he boomed, making himself heard despite the noise from the chopper. We met, shook hands and hugged each other.

'I am so very sorry about what happened this morning, Frank.'

'Me, too, not that it was your fault.' I shrugged. 'What's the news of Charles?'

'The doctors believe he will live. That is the main news.'

'Thank God!' I said with relief.

'As for his injuries, and how he will be in future, they say it is too soon to tell. They have done what they can for the moment. He is in an induced coma now, and must be allowed to rest if the healing process is to begin.'

'These are your doctors — at your hospital?'

'The Medical Centre. Yes. They are very good people there, the best. And we must leave them to do their work.

'Come! Let us go inside. Lenka will join us when she has shut down the helicopter.'

* * *

We settled in a comfortable living room and Leon found us a couple of bottles of a very good Czech pilsener. While he was opening them, Věra reappeared. She told him something important in a Slavonic language that sounded to me like Czech. Not Russian, anyway. He nodded and thanked her. She left.

'Our evening meal will be ready in thirty minutes,' Leon informed me. 'Věra will not tolerate us being late for it,' he added gravely.

'I understand.' I smiled and added, 'Domestic arrangements are very important, Leon. You're lucky to have someone here who makes you respect them.'

'I agree,' he responded, with a mischievous twinkle in his eye.

'Now tell me what the hell happened this morning,' I suggested. 'Was that reception for me?'

'At this moment, I can't be sure. All I can tell you is how much I regret you were put through such an ordeal.'

'And Charles, and the men who died,' I pointed out. 'I got out of it lightly.'

'Of course. It was a very bad morning for many people.'

'The other side lost men, too.'

Leon shrugged.

'But you don't know who they were?'

He shook his head. 'We have an idea, and we will find out for sure, but right now I would only be guessing. It is better to wait to say more until I am certain.'

It was a fair point, but I wasn't sure I agreed with him. Sometimes speculation throws up answers. In any case, knowing him, I guessed that he already knew more than he was telling me.

'Had you been expecting something like that to happen? Was that why you wanted me here?'

'No, no, of course not! You are here for another reason. I will tell you more about that in the morning, when we are both fresh. For now, I will say only what you already know. I wanted you here to protect Olga.

'You are my friend, Frank. I trust you. Also, I know what your capabilities are. You can do what no one else could do. That is all I wish to say for now.'

'Fair enough.'

It wasn't, of course. I still knew next to nothing. But I knew better than to press him further. That would do no good. He would just take refuge in endless obfuscation, and probably lapse into another of his many languages, leaving me floundering and frustrated.

'Will there be difficulties with the police after this morning's events?' I asked.

'Difficulties? There are always difficulties!' he said with a chuckle. 'What do you mean, Frank?'

'Oh, you know. Removing people from a major crime scene by helicopter, interfering in that scene, and being in some way responsible for it. And you a Russian émigré, of course.'

He shrugged. 'I think not. At least, those are difficulties that can be overcome. I am not unknown to the police and security people in this country. They know exactly who I am, and what I do — some of it, at least. Yet I am still welcome here, I believe.

'Apart from being a Czech citizen and contributing to the Czech economy, there are people in government who value my contacts in the Russian Federation and elsewhere in eastern Europe. Sometimes — quite often, actually — governments depend on what the Americans call backchannels to communicate and negotiate with each other in private.'

I knew that to be true, even for governments that in public hated each other. My belief was that Leon did quite a lot of that behind-the-scenes stuff. People like him, with language skills, experience of life in other countries and the ability to move effortlessly across national borders without comment have always been much needed.

Civil servants are the Sherpas who set things up and make the arrangements for formal meetings and discussions, but before they can enter the scene, others are needed to make overtures and prepare the ground before anything at all can be discussed between governments that don't see eye to eye. That's how it is, and always has been.

'Even so, Leon,' I said doggedly, thinking it couldn't be that simple — it just couldn't! 'What happened this morning can't be hushed up as a private matter. It affected too many people.'

'It won't be hushed up. Already it is front-page news and on the TV screens. People are chattering about it on social media. I believe the consensus will be that it was a terrorist incident. Nothing else. Which, of course, is exactly what it was.'

He had me there. A terrorist incident? Of course it was! And he was no more to blame for it than any other innocent target of a bomb or outbreak of wild shooting. In the eyes of the sensible world, that is. Only conspiracy enthusiasts were likely to differ.

'Besides,' he added, with a twinkle in his eye, 'I have a very good friend in Prague.'

'Oh? And who might that be?'

'The president.'

'The president, huh?'

I was more impressed than I wanted to admit. I had long known Leon's considerable political reach, but even so . . .

'How do you know him?'

'He is a businessman, like me,' Leon said airily. 'And he is not prejudiced against all people from Russia. He grew up alongside us, and even went to the University of Moscow.'

'Nice to know.'

'Also,' Leon said with a chuckle, 'I bought his old house, paying him a lot more than it was worth.'

Ah! I had to smile at that.

'Not . . . Not this house?'

He nodded.

'Yes, this house. The location and other things about it suited me very well, and he wanted rid of it. His ancestor had built the house, and it had been in his family for generations, but his new, young second wife didn't like it. She wanted to live somewhere modern. Actually, I was able to help him with that, as well.'

'More fool him — and her!' I said, laughing and shaking my head. 'This is a wonderful house.'

'I think so, too. It was a very good investment.'

In more ways than one, I couldn't help thinking. This was realpolitik — the way of the world. I had read that the Czech president had recently been re-elected for another term. So that had effectively given Leon another five years of personal and political backing at the heart of Czech government.

Paying over the odds for the president's old house had probably not been the only contribution Leon had made to his electoral campaign, either. I wouldn't have been too surprised to learn that Leon had actually built the new house for him, as well.

Mind you, he had probably contributed to the election campaign of the president's main rival, as well. You can't be too careful when you're looking to the future.

Before I could ask a supplementary question, the door opened and Lenka entered the room.

'Frank!' she cried, wearing a smile not often seen on that so-very-serious face. 'You came to visit us again? I am so pleased.'

'I couldn't stay away, Lenka. I tried, but I just couldn't.'

'Welcome back!'

* * *

I can't say we spent a convivial evening, chez Leon. It had been an exceptionally bad day for us all, and feelings were very raw. I was battered and bruised myself, both physically and mentally, and Lenka was understandably tired and in need of rest after some intense flying around the city.

As for Leon, he still had plenty to do and many phone calls to make. I guessed there would be police and intelligence officials to satisfy and politicos to placate — notwithstanding his optimism. Then there would be medics to liaise with about Charles. After the day's events, there would also be arrangements to make for fallen comrades and gaps in his organisation to refill. I didn't envy him.

So, good as it was to catch up with Leon and Lenka again, and to share a meal with them, I soon left them to it and sought an early night. After another shower and donning some fresh clothes that Věra had miraculously found in my size, I left the lights off in my room and sat by the window for a while, gazing out into the night.

Needless to say, it wasn't a dark sky out there, not in a city of one and a half million people, but the lights stretching away into the distance were a pleasant novelty for me. You can't see much at night from my cottage at Risky Point. Next to nothing, usually, unless there's a full moon.

The lights here were comforting. On this little hill, amid the beautiful grounds of this old house, I felt above the terrible events of the morning. Safe, too. Ironic for a security consultant to feel like that, and to welcome the feeling, but I did. Despite not having seen any evidence of security provision, I knew we would be well protected by the best people and equipment available. Leon always did things well. False optimism on my part, perhaps, but it was enough to make me feel better.

My thoughts returned to Charles, and how he had sacrificed himself to protect me. That didn't make me feel good, but there was nothing I could do about it now, except salute the man and hope he pulled through. Then I thought of the third Podolsky sibling, Olga, and wondered where and how she was. So far, there had been only the briefest passing mention of her. Yet she seemed to be the reason I was here.

An extraordinarily gentle woman possessed of exceptional abilities, it was always here, in this house, that she stood whenever I pictured Olga. This was where she and I had first spoken at any length, and the ambience and mood of the house had seemed to suit her so very well. She was not a modern young woman in any respect, but her work, which was IT-based, and this place suited her perfectly. Here, she moved quietly, effortlessly through the stillness as if she had been part of the house ever since it had been built.

Obviously, she was not here now. She would have appeared to greet me by now if she had been. I regretted her absence. I missed her calming presence. In an earlier age, she was a woman who might have founded a religious establishment and presided over it to the joy of all who came across her. That was just how she was.

CHAPTER TWENTY-ONE

Surprisingly, perhaps, I slept well. The ancient, watchful presence of the house seemed to have a settling influence on all who entered. Even the owner of the house seemed less manic when he was here.

After breakfast the next morning, Leon and I got down to business, and the reason I was in Prague. It was time. Yesterday was done. Now we moved on.

We took extra cups of coffee with us and adjourned from the dining room to Leon's office. We sat in upright but comfortable chairs arranged around an old table that might have been created for the Habsburgs in the halcyon days of the Austro-Hungarian Empire, of which Prague and Bohemia had been an integral part.

My opening gambit was: 'You have so much security here, Leon, that I can't imagine why you felt you needed me, as well.'

'You bring something extra to the table, Frank. Always. Ever since that first day outside the hotel, when you helped me fight back against the gang that had attacked me. I need that resolve and strength again right now, for the next few weeks or so especially.'

He was referring to our initial encounter outside the so-called boutique hotel he owned in the city, where I had just happened to be staying on a short-break city holiday. I had stepped outside for a breath of fresh air and immediately found myself amid a street battle, with a group of toughs attacking one man. The man was putting up a valiant fight, but he was outnumbered, near the end of his strength, and going down. I'd had no idea who he was, but instinct kicked in, and, unthinkingly, I waded in to help him. He had never let me forget it.

It was only afterwards, when he was expressing his gratitude, that I discovered he was called Leon Podolsky, and that he owned the hotel, as well as much else. After that, I did some security work for him, and we got to know each other pretty well as a result. We had helped each other out in other difficult situations, and an unlikely friendship between us had grown. I had come to know him as a good man who lived life on the edge, a brother in arms — but one on a much sharper edge, on a much higher mountain, than me, and with a lot bigger drop below him.

'A few weeks, or so, Leon? You have a situation here that will be resolved in that time?'

'I believe so. It is a difficult situation, but it must be dealt with by then.'

'How does Olga come into it?'

'I want you to look out for her.'

'So you said. Has something happened to her?'

'Not yet, thank God,' he said, shaking his head. 'But she is very much at risk, now more than usual.'

It was a relief to hear she was all right at present.

'I will do what I can to help, Leon. Where is she, for a start? Northumberland?'

He shook his head. 'If she were there, Frank, I wouldn't have brought you to Prague, would I?' He smiled.

I had asked the question because the Podolsky empire used to have one of its IT bases in the north of the county, largely because of Olga. She had identified a big old house there, The Chesters, as a suitable location for doing some of the IT work she was responsible for. Then she had fallen in love with the sad, semi-derelict, old place and committed herself to restoring it.

Sadly, an arson attack had destroyed the house, but Olga had recovered from that blow and rebuilt it. Doing so had only really made sense if you were of a romantic, sentimental disposition. Olga was certainly that, notwithstanding her career and skills in the IT world.

Her life was a balancing act. She had found a way of fitting her different sides together seemingly without friction. I envied her, as well as respected her. She was a very special person.

'You'd better tell me more,' I suggested.

Leon began slowly. 'Olga has special abilities, as you know very well, Frank. They make her highly valuable, but also highly vulnerable. The Podolsky family business would find it difficult, almost impossible, to cope without her. Olga is essential to us, and my rivals and enemies know that. It is what makes her so vulnerable.

'She is also much loved for herself, of course,' he added. 'But I don't need to tell you that.'

I shook my head, knowing full well what the family thought of Olga. I had seen the Podolskys prepared to move heaven and earth to get her back when she had once been abducted.

'Has something happened, Leon?'

'She is fine right now. Just the same as usual.'

'But something has happened?'

'There have been . . . indications, shall we say? And there are possibilities.'

Veiled threats, perhaps? Signs that something was afoot? Leon's intelligence network would pick up things that had to be considered, however remote or flimsy they were.

'And right now,' he continued, 'especially after events at the airport yesterday, there is more to worry about than usual.'

'Where is she?'

'She lives in a small village in the countryside, in Northern Bohemia. You remember how she likes simple, traditional things? Old buildings, fields and forest, vases of dried flowers — all that?'

I nodded, but declined to be deflected. 'Where exactly, Leon?'

'Kámen, the village is called.'

'Where is it?'

'Not far from Děčín. Do you know that city? Probably not, no.'

I frowned, thinking, trying to remember. There was something about the name . . . Ah!

'Yes, I do actually. Some years ago I was there, briefly. One of those places that the Germans, who used to live there before World War II, had a different name for. Tetschen, or something like that.'

Leon smiled. 'You surprise me, Frank. You are very well informed, and travelled.'

'Not really. And I don't know Kámen at all.'

'Not many people do. It is not much. Very small. And insignificant. That is why Olga is there. She likes such places. Her choice,' he added with a shrug. 'Not mine.'

He shook his head, as if bewildered, and paused for a moment.

'So she is not here,' he resumed. 'She is somewhere she prefers.'

Then he looked at me and added, 'But she was to have met you yesterday at the airport.'

Ah! I grimaced at the thought of how that might have worked out.

'I believe the people who made the attack were not really aiming at you at all,' Leon continued. 'Olga was their target. That is what is so worrying. Somehow they knew she was supposed to be there.

'She wanted to meet you, to welcome you back to this country, and she was looking forward to it very much. But a minor illness meant it was better for her to stay at home. She didn't want to do that, but I insisted. I said you would be with her soon enough.

'That turns out to have been something of a blessing — for her, at least.'

He mused for a moment, and then said, 'So will you take the job, Frank?'

'Of course,' I assured him. 'It's why I'm here.'

'Good. There is no one else acceptable to Olga. She absolutely refuses to have anyone else I have suggested.'

I nodded. My brain was already racing through the gears, assessing the situation as well as I could on the basis of the limited information I'd been given. There was a threat to Olga, and for some reason, time was of the essence. That just about summed it up. The length of time Leon was talking about suited me well enough. I couldn't have committed to a stay without end.

'The attack at the airport, Leon. Do you know any more about it yet?'

'Not really. But we will soon enough,' he assured me once again.

'Was it politically motivated, do you think? Or was it for business reasons?'

He just shrugged.

'When the trouble started in Ukraine, Leon, I wondered where you would stand, and if it would affect you.'

'And what did you decide?'

'I believed you would find the invasion unacceptable, and that you would find ways of making that clear, even if it was dangerous. Was I right?'

'Of course,' he said with another shrug. 'But I didn't have to do much. Not being sanctioned by the EU, or by the West in general, was enough for the Kremlin to bracket me with the enemy.'

'Has your business been affected?'

'Not by sanctions. But in other ways, of course. Just like most businesses everywhere. As the experts keep telling us, we have a global economy these days.'

He paused there to think about something before continuing.

'My business interests are not so important anyway, when it comes to the war in Ukraine. More significant is my own personal background.'

I'd wondered about that, too. He'd never told me much about his life before serving as a special forces officer, a spetsnaz, in the Russian army.

'What am I?' he asked dramatically. 'Russian? Well, perhaps. In a sense. I grew up in Moscow. But my mother was Ukrainian, my father from Moldova, and I was actually born in Tbilisi, Georgia. So a bit of a wanderer, as so many were in the Soviet Union.

'Not that any of that matters much now. I simply believe that Putin has taken Russia in the wrong direction ever since he came to power, and as a result, everyone suffers.

'So,' he added dismissively, 'I do what little I can to help Volodymyr Zelensky, and poor old Ukraine. You might think that would make me a target for the Russian intelligence services, and my sisters with me, but the reality is that they have too much to do and think about to be worried about the Podolsky family.'

He was probably right about that, I thought.

'I will do what I can for Olga,' I told him.

He nodded and gave me a wry smile and a pat on the back. 'I never doubted it, Frank.'

I left for Kámen later that morning. The thirteenth of November.

CHAPTER TWENTY-TWO

Prague
13 November

Kravertz took only Jed Smith with him when he flew to Prague. There were others he could have taken as well, but not many he could fully trust. Jed was his main man, and they were in this together. They had a mutual interest in sorting things out. Besides, there was a lot going on in the North Sea and back at Haverton Hill. People left behind had plenty to do. Fifty-year-old oil rigs didn't demolish themselves. They needed a bit of help.

He sat by himself on the plane from Newcastle, wanting space and time to himself to pull things together in his head. Jed was OK with that. He was used to how he was, and realised he had a lot to consider, some of it difficult.

No way could he have refused to do what Manny wanted, but having to accept the order he'd been given about priorities had made things more complicated. Manny wanted the Russian woman eliminated, and that to be the priority. Kravertz had had to accept that. At the same time, he hadn't liked the idea of having to back off from the hunt for Burke. Nor had he appreciated the statement that Burke was his problem alone, and nothing to do with the Brotherhood. That had stuck in his craw.

So far as he was concerned, they were in all of this together, whatever Manny thought. If Burke had his day in court, assuming the investigation of KOSC ever got that far, it wouldn't be only him, Daniel Kravertz, losing out. KOSC itself would be brought down. And then the Brotherhood would lose their investment, which had certainly not been trivial. He had to wonder why Manny, or somebody else back there in Wall Street, or wherever the hell they were based, couldn't see that.

He stopped and put the lid on that kind of thinking. It was too dangerous. If things ever did get to court, he might need Manny and the Brotherhood to find and pay for lawyers to keep him out of jail for the rest of his life.

All because of that bloody Burke! He ground his teeth and snarled inwardly. How he regretted taking Burke with them when he and Jed went to sort out the divers. He'd believed by then that he could trust him, that he was on their side after all they had done for him. Boy, had he got that wrong! Badly wrong! So maybe Manny was justified, to some extent, in telling him it was his problem, not theirs, to sort out.

He put all that out of his mind when he heard the pilot telling air crew they would be landing in Prague in fifteen minutes. It was time to think about the Czechs who Manny had arranged to meet and help him.

CHAPTER TWENTY-THREE

Kámen, Northern Bohemia

Lenka flew me in her helicopter to a small airport favoured by the military a short distance from Prague. I had been there with Leon once before, and I knew he liked it for the same reasons as the military did. Security was good and it was well run, being kept open in all weathers and in all circumstances.

There, I picked up a Skoda Yeti, the popular Czech SUV. Departing that way meant that anyone who might have been watching Leon's house wouldn't know where I'd gone or what vehicle I was driving. Given what had already happened since my arrival, it seemed a sensible precaution to take.

I could have been flown further, but I wanted physical separation from Lenka and Leon, lest anyone monitoring them would be inadvertently led to Olga. Also, I needed time to re-acclimatise to the country and to think through what I was going to be doing. A little relaxation wouldn't go amiss, either. The drive through the Czech countryside would allow me that, and would only take a couple of hours. Time well spent, even if my mission was urgent.

* * *

Kámen didn't look much, when I got there. It certainly wasn't pretty as a postcard. Nothing like that. It was just a tired-looking, run-down old street village. Most of the houses were on the main road that climbed up the gently sloping hill, and in a few more miles took the traveller to the border with Saxony. I drove to the top of the hill, where the road disappeared into dense forest, and then turned round and came back down again. I wasn't looking for the address I had for Olga yet. I just wanted an initial overview of the village, and to get a first impression.

What I saw at first was a lot of very old, traditional houses in varying states of repair, their walls in some cases literally coming up to the road's edge, leaving no space for a footpath. There would have been a time when motorised traffic was so infrequent that passing vehicles would have been more of an interesting novelty than a nuisance, but that was long ago. Now, every time a truck roared past, there was a good chance that more render, or plaster skim, would fall from the timber-frame buildings.

Behind the main street I could see a scatter of modern houses, some big and very new. No doubt money from the nearby city of Děčín was moving in, the people bringing it requiring modern facilities as well as rural living. In that respect, it would be the same here as everywhere else these days, including the old ironstone mining villages of my home patch in Cleveland.

Kámen didn't seem to be much of a service centre. There was a traditional pub-restaurant at the bottom of the hill, and I spotted one or two little convenience shops operating out of what looked like the front rooms of ordinary houses. There was also an old garage with a couple of pumps on the fore-court, one for petrol and the other for diesel, or benzín and nafta, respectively, as the Czechs have it. And a cemetery. No church, though. Perhaps that was lost, like so many others, during the decades of Communist government. And that was it. What more could a little village want anyway?

Olga's house was at the end of a track off the main road, and set back a couple of hundred yards. It was not one of the modern buildings. On the contrary, to my uneducated eye when it came to Czech architecture, it looked very ancient. It also looked very tired, fast heading towards being a ruin, as if its drooping, decaying timbers were feeling their age and about to give up.

How very Olga, I couldn't help thinking with a smile, as I drove along the short drive of bare earth and compressed cinders, and drew up close to the house. She spends her working hours in ultra-modern mode, working with hi-tec equipment in the world of global finance, but chooses to live as if the twentieth century, never mind the twenty-first, hasn't yet arrived.

As I got out and closed the car door after me, the front door of the house opened and Olga came out to greet me. She looked just as I remembered her. Medium height, a little plump, shoulder-length brown hair, and a smile to capture the heart of all whose hearts are not made of stone.

With a little skip, she hurried towards me, arms held out wide. I laughed and met her halfway. We hugged and then stepped back to gaze at each other.

'Dear Frank,' she said softly. 'It is so good to see you again after all this time.'

'That's exactly how I feel about you, Olga. How are you?'

'I am very well, thank you. But, Frank, you look tired, so tired! What has been happening to you?'

'Nothing much. I've just been busy. That's all.'

'Doing the same things?'

'Oh, yes. My life is much the same. I'm not like you, Olga, moving between cities, and between countries, all the time.'

'Oh, but my work is the same.'

'With the computers?'

'Yes. I do the same things.'

'Yet you always have an interesting project on the go, as well. I know you! In England, it was the old house you renovated, and then had to rebuild after the fire.'

With a smile, she said, 'Yes, you are right, Frank. Always I have some little hobby. There, it was The Chesters, the ancient stone house.'

'I wonder what it is here?'

I shaded my eyes with one hand and peered around dramatically, as if I couldn't already see an old house in urgent need of some care and attention.

She laughed. Then she took my hand and led me inside.

CHAPTER TWENTY-FOUR

Prague

The Czechs were waiting for Kravertz and Smith at the airport. Introductions made, they were quickly got outside and into a couple of vehicles. Then they sped to some unknown part of an unknown city, so far as Kravertz was concerned. They were taken into an old warehouse, where an upstairs mezzanine formed residential accommodation.

'Nice,' Kravertz said, trying to hide his disdain as he looked around at what seemed to be a big living room.

'We like it,' said Zeman, the gang leader, a tough-looking man with a commanding personality.

'I can see why. You're well hidden. No one would think of looking for you here, in an industrial district.'

Zeman chuckled. 'No one,' he agreed.

Invited to do so, Kravertz and Smith sat down on one of several long sofas in the room. Zeman and three of his men sat down on another, a big coffee table between the two parties.

'Do you have news for us?' Kravertz asked, as another man served coffee.

'Yes, but it is not good news,' Zeman said with a shrug. 'I had hoped to be able to tell you that your journey had not been necessary, and that you could go back home immediately.'

'That's more or less what I was told to hope for,' Kravertz said.

'By Mr Mannheim?'

Kravertz nodded. 'So what happened?'

'We made an attack just outside the airport, but unfortunately the target escaped. My men never found her.'

'That's too bad.'

'It is. And I lost several good men, two dead and three badly wounded.'

'I'm sorry to hear it. Please accept my condolences.'

Zeman bowed his head, in acknowledgement.

Kravertz processed the news and ran through things fast, feeling thoroughly pissed off. It meant they were going to have to stay in this goddam country longer than he'd hoped. That was the only clear conclusion he reached.

'But we still must move forward, Mr Zeman. At least, I must. Mr Mannheim expects no less of me. Are you able to offer us any hope for the future?'

'Yes. There is much I can tell you, and there are things we can do together.' He chuckled and added, 'Mr Mannheim is our big boss, eh? We must not disappoint him.'

'I can see you and I are on the same page, Mr Zeman. That's good to know.'

'Milan,' Zeman said. 'I am Milan Zeman.'

'And I am Daniel, Daniel Kravertz.'

'It is good,' Zeman said with more warmth.

Jed Smith, speaking for the first time, was practical as ever. 'Where will we stay?'

'Oh, we have rooms for special guests like you. Come!'

Zeman led them up on to another floor and along a corridor lined by doors opening into small rooms with bunk beds.

'Each room has its own bathroom,' Zeman said proudly. 'Five-star accommodation, eh?'

'Very much so,' Kravertz said, glancing around askance at the room he was evidently to share with Smith.

It was not what he had expected, or was used to, but he refrained from expressing his true feelings. He needed Zeman and his outfit if he and Smith were to accomplish what they had come to do. Besides, Manny had set this up, and he had no wish to irritate him further. The business with Burke was bad enough. Hopefully, they wouldn't be here long anyway.

Jed was looking at him pointedly, no doubt expecting to hear some sort of complaint about the accommodation.

Kravertz smiled, saying, 'This is just what we need, Jed.'

For a moment, Smith seemed poised to disagree. The moment passed. 'Perfect,' he said, nodding with feigned approval.

* * *

'What do you think, boss?' Smith asked, as soon as they were left alone.

'About what?'

Smith shrugged. 'You know — them.'

'They seem OK to me. Something bothering you?'

Smith grimaced. 'For a start, I can't understand a single fucking thing they say to each other.'

Kravertz laughed. 'The perils of foreign travel, Jed!'

'Well, I've been to Benidorm and Rhodes. The foreigners there were all right. They spoke our language. I didn't have any problems. I didn't in Magaluf, either,' he added.

'Don't let it worry you, Jed. Look, we're here because Manny set it up for us. He knows these guys. It seems he's worked with them before. So they must be good at what they do. He trusts them. And that's good enough for me.'

Smith nodded and wandered over to a little window overlooking a lot of industrial roof space, and not much else.

Kravertz slung his bag on to one of the lower-level bunks, lay down and closed his eyes. He had some thinking to do.

'That's another thing,' Smith said suddenly. 'Manny. Who is he? What is he? You've never said much about him.'

'Just my contact man with the organisation. That's all. He's a member of the inner circle, and he's the one who deals with me. So far as KOSC is concerned, and you and me, Jed, he's Mr Everything. KOSC wouldn't exist without him.'

Smith chewed that over and then said, 'You don't deal with anyone else in the organisation?'

'No.'

'Never?'

'What is this?' Kravertz said, sitting up sharply. 'An interrogation? For Chrissake, Jed! Don't make me regret bringing you.'

'Sorry, boss,' Smith said apologetically. 'I was just wondering. That's all.'

'Well, you'd better stop it. We came here to do a job. Let's get it done, using the people Manny gave us, and then get the hell out of here.'

'OK.'

'Agreed?'

'Agreed.'

CHAPTER TWENTY-FIVE

Kámen, Northern Bohemia

Olga's flat in Prague, when and where I first met her, had been like a museum. It was in an old, run-down building in an old, shabby part of the city, and it was furnished to match. For authenticity, I suppose. I recalled furniture and panelling with wood so dark it was almost black. And there was brocade and leather, Turkish rugs on wooden floors, huge vases containing dried flowers, ancient pictures of countryside scenes in summer and winter: haystacks, windmills and long-ago people skating on frozen ponds.

The house in Kámen, I soon realised, was just like that flat, only much, much bigger, and fuller. I knew why, or believed I did. Like the flat in Prague and The Chesters in Northumberland, this house was Olga's escape from the contemporary world, where she spent her working days. It was how she brought the balance into her life that she hadn't had during her years in California, or since then in Europe.

In short, it was the very opposite of Silicon Valley, where she must have been so uncomfortable in a personal sense, but that had been so essential and rewarding in terms of her professional development. It wasn't Russia either, where she had originally come from, but it was still part of the Slavonic world to which she felt she belonged.

The big kitchen was the hub of the house and that was where we settled, at a farmhouse table, when Olga led me indoors. It was an old-fashioned kitchen, of course, lacking the influence of a contemporary designer, or the plastic, glass and stainless steel to be seen in the pictures of kitchens in glossy magazines. I liked it, and felt at home there. It reminded me of her old flat in Prague, and it wasn't much different from my own kitchen back in Risky Point.

'Will you have coffee with me, Frank?' Olga asked in her endearing way, as if my acceptance would do her an enormous favour.

I nodded, smiled and said, 'I would like that very much. Thank you.'

While she made and poured the coffee, I glanced around approvingly at the bunches of dried flowers in a variety of containers, not only vases, and at bunches of drying herbs, hanging from hooks in ceiling beams. There were also clumps of onions and garlic up there, too, all contributing to the rich aroma that filled the kitchen.

'You must have a vegetable garden, a kitchen garden?' I suggested.

She followed my eyes and nodded. 'Oh, yes. A small one. I like to grow at least some of my own food. And looking after the plants is healthy for me, as well as something I enjoy doing.'

I nodded. I could understand all that.

'How long have you lived here?'

'For some time,' she said equivocally, giving little away. 'It is good for me to be here.'

'I'm sure it is. This is a fine old house, Olga.'

'The village is fine, too.'

Hmm? I wondered about that. I really did, from what I'd seen of it.

'How did you find Kámen?'

'I didn't, Frank. Kámen found me,' she said with a smile. 'I believe you will understand, when I say that?'

Strangely enough, I did. Or thought I did. The explanation fitted well with how I thought of Olga. That was how she was. Dreamy and romantic.

Not everything can, or could, be explained. Some things, some parts of her life, she kept to herself. I didn't begrudge her that. Nor did the other members of her family, from what I'd seen. Olga was special. We all knew that. Not normal, perhaps, although I hesitate to say that, but very special.

Cleverer people than me might have a name for it, the name of some syndrome or other to explain hyperintelligence and great sensitivity. Perhaps it's even a form of autism. I don't know. For me, and her family, it was just how she was: Olga. No need for further explanation. No need at all.

* * *

Even so, respectful as I was of her way of life, I needed to stake out some territory for myself. I had a job to do.

'Have you had any difficulty while you've been here, Olga? Have there been any threats, or has anything happened to upset you?'

She frowned as she thought about that. 'No direct threats, Frank. But I know that my brother is concerned about my safety. It is why you are here, yes?'

I nodded. 'Yes. Leon thinks you are at serious risk.'

'Because of what I do for the family business.'

'Especially now, Olga. Because Leon regards me as a friend, and knows what I do for a living, he has asked me to join you for a short time.'

She nodded, looking very thoughtful. 'Leon thinks very highly of you, Frank, and he trusts you. So do I.'

'Thank you, Olga!' I grinned and added, 'That's the nicest thing anyone has said to me for a long time.'

'I am sure that is not true!' She smiled and said, 'But you must do what is necessary here, and I will not be in your way.

Live here, as if it is your own home. And when we are not working, I hope you will permit me to show you the garden, and the village?'

'Of course.'

'Now, if you have finished your coffee, I will show you to your room and take you round the rest of the house.'

CHAPTER TWENTY-SIX

I got outside as soon as I could after she had shown me around the house, leaving Olga to get on with her work.

Then I checked my phone, which was muted, and found I had a couple of voicemail messages. One was from Bill Peart, saying he was very worried and needed to talk to me again about the Jamie Burke situation. I grimaced, and wished I'd not bothered with voicemail or the phone. I wasn't on holiday, but I was away, far away. There wasn't much I could do about things back at home.

The other message was from Jimmy Mack. He knew where I was, and had my phone number. He'd called to say Bill Peart had been looking for me urgently, and seemed stressed about something.

I sighed. But I couldn't ignore Bill. I ought to at least let him know that I was unavailable. So I called him on his personal phone. No way did I want anything we said recorded automatically on a police computer, which I assumed would be what happened.

'Thanks for getting back to me, Frank. I wanted to have a word with you about Jamie Burke. He's the lad who quit Witness Protection, who . . .'

'I know who he is, Bill. I've actually met him, and talked to him.'

'Oh?'

'A mutual friend asked me to look in on him, thinking he might like some company. He lives not far from Risky Point. What's the problem? Is he all right?'

'As far as I know, he is. The thing is, we've not been able to catch up with him for a day or two. Nobody has seen anything of him. So I don't really know, but I'm worried about him. That's what I wanted to talk to you about.

'As you know, we're supposed to be keeping an eye on him, but it's proving very difficult. About all we can do is cruise past his house and occasionally check to see if he's there. Or give him a phone call from time to time. But he doesn't want us to call him every day.

'Now he's not there, though. He seems to be missing. I wondered if you might have any ideas?'

I grimaced. It didn't sound good.

'I can't see what else you can do, Bill. Except speak to the woman next door. Jenny, she's called. See if she knows anything. Apparently, they're on friendly terms.'

'Done that. She doesn't.'

'Well, it's up to him to call you, isn't it, if there's a problem? Maybe he's just visiting someone?'

'Mmm.'

He was obviously hoping for a better suggestion than that, but I didn't have one to offer. Besides, I wasn't there, and I had enough here to think about.

'Sorry, Bill. I haven't got anything else to suggest. I'm not at home right now, either. I'm away on a job.'

'Where?'

'Abroad, Bill. I'm in foreign parts.'

'Where the sun never stops shining, I suppose?'

'And the beer never stops flowing!' I assured him.

'Ah! Not wine country, then?'

'Oh, they've got that, as well.'

* * *

There, we left it. I had nothing more of value to contribute about Jamie Burke, much as I would have liked to help Bill. There wasn't anything I could do to help Jamie, either.

I got back to my current job, protecting Olga. The attack at the airport made more sense now that Leon had told me he believed Olga was the target, not me. I hadn't been able to understand why anyone in Prague could be after me, and it was a relief to learn that probably no one was.

But the update had made me more concerned about Olga. If she'd been there, they could have hit her just outside the Vaclav Havel Airport, with all its security. So why not here in this sleepy little village?

Obviously, I needed to check out Olga's supposedly safe base, and identify its vulnerabilities as a matter of urgency.

Despite its external appearance, the house was a lovely old place on the inside. It really was. As Olga showed me around, I had been able to understand how it had appealed to her. Ancient rooms, some long left to slumber unoccupied and unused, perhaps even forgotten. Little windows, through which light full of dusty sunbeams slanted at different angles according to the time of day. Ancient staircases and corridors that creaked as we passed up and along them.

It was a big house, too, as well as a very old one. My guess was that, until Olga arrived, it had long been little used, if not entirely abandoned. Part of its attraction for her was probably that she had relished the opportunity to save it from becoming a total ruin. It had been like that with The Chesters. I shook my head and smiled at that memory. What a romantic she was!

Now this house was being awakened from its slumbers and given a new lease of life. There were signs everywhere of Olga's presence. Floors had been swept and windows cleaned. Although some rooms were disused and empty still, others had been cleaned and furnished with beds, chairs, tables and chests of drawers appropriate to the age of the house.

There were ancient pictures hanging on walls, too, some looking as if they had always belonged there, others suggesting it had been Olga that had found and brought them to a place where they fitted perfectly. I wondered where everything had come from. Skips, junk shops, abandoned houses, museums? Probably. All of them, no doubt.

Olga had spoken of her renovation plans, but so far only a new bathroom and the computer room, which filled virtually the entire basement, spoke of modernity. Only there did I see age-inappropriate furnishings and banks of gleaming modern machines and equipment, as well as very bright lighting, to confirm that Olga was still in the IT business.

I didn't venture very far inside the computer room. One glance was enough for me. I glimpsed it from the doorway and turned away, repelled by the flashing screens, unceasing chatter of the machines and the hum of the vigorous ventilation system needed to keep them all cool. Such modernity felt like an insult to the house.

Apart from the basement, the house looked lovely to my eyes, as it obviously did to Olga's. Here, just as at Chesters, she had seen something to settle into and cherish, as well as a place where she could pursue her work uninterrupted. I assumed she planned to restore the whole house eventually, but that was going to take some considerable time.

All that, I could see and understand. But after my first circuit, the house also worried me a lot. From a security point of view, it was a disaster waiting to happen. This was no place for Olga to be, given the calibre of the people hunting her. It was a potential death trap.

For a start, it was an ancient timber structure, built of wood that had dried out centuries ago. Admittedly, it had been built on a stone base, but the tinder-dry superstructure was not capable of stopping bullets and was likely to go up in a ball of flame if anybody started shooting at it, or even got too close with a lighted match.

I exaggerate — but not by much. Olga would have been far safer in Prague, in a modern block of flats built of concrete and steel, or in one of the ancient stone-built mansions in that same city. Her brother's hotel, or his house, even. But that wasn't how and where she had chosen to live.

I didn't envy Leon. Long term, he had his work cut out trying to protect her, along with everything else he had to do, and for him it was a lifetime commitment. Me? I only had to do it for two or three weeks, hopefully.

Anyway, that was the house. There were a few things I could do, and others I could tweak, that would help, but they wouldn't amount to very much. Not if we were up against the people who had launched the attack in Prague. The old house could never be converted into a fortress.

I soon decided the best idea was to try to persuade Olga to leave and return to Prague. But I knew she wouldn't contemplate doing that. I would be wasting my breath. All I would get in return would be a beatific smile that would melt the hearts of angels, but not of Leon's enemies and rivals.

The grounds of the house offered some opportunities for a defensive upgrade, not least because the property was a good size for a traditional village setting. It was a couple of acres in size, say 100 yards by 300, a big piece of land if you thought of it as a garden. From what I'd seen, many properties in the village were a good size. My guess was that traditionally each one had been the Czech equivalent of a smallholding. People could have produced much of their own food from crops and livestock, and then had a surplus they could take to market or use to barter.

The traditional smallholdings and family farms had been largely obliterated in Czechoslovakia at the start of the Communist era, but property boundaries had not been lost or forgotten. Eventually, when that era came to an end, the original owners or their descendants had returned to reclaim their rights, and many small property holdings like this one had been recreated through the restitution laws.

The land around Olga's house had never been a garden. It was too big for that. Much of it was now more of a meadow, a field of wild grass with a scatter of fruit trees and a couple of big old conifers. Paths had been worn or cut through the grass recently, but most of it would have been waist-high in summer. Close to the house, there were flowering shrubs and the small vegetable bed Olga had mentioned.

That was about it. The property was mostly an empty field. I walked around the boundary, trying to identify potential weak and strong points. Then I made my way through the grassland, checking the ground and finding nothing special about it. Just a lot of dead grass, clay and mud now, following the autumn chill and rains. There wasn't anything I hadn't been able to see from the edges of the field.

There were two big sheds near the house. One was in use as a garage, housing a little Skoda car that I assumed belonged to Olga. The other held garden tools and a few bags of stuff, including fertiliser and cement, that looked to have been there a long time.

My preliminary survey took half an hour. Afterwards, I sat on the porch steps at the front of the house and thought about what it might be possible to do. A few defensive measures could be introduced, but some would take a lot longer than others to construct or put in place. I had to be realistic about what could be done in the time I was supposed to be here.

Something else to bear in mind was that whatever was done here ought not to be controversial or grandiose. We didn't want the whole village wondering what was going on, and risk attracting the interest of people hunting Olga.

After doing and thinking all that, I went to talk to the lady of the house again.

CHAPTER TWENTY-SEVEN

'How long have you lived here, Olga?'

'In Kámen?'

'Yes.'

'For one year. Since we bought this house. Leon did not tell you?'

I shook my head.

She smiled fondly and said, 'My brother doesn't like me living here.'

'I gathered that.'

She turned back to the stove, where she was cooking what she said would be a celebratory meal to herald my arrival, something I really didn't deserve, in my opinion.

I was thinking. A whole year? Plenty long enough for the powers of darkness to have found her. It might have taken them a while, but a year was surely more than enough. It's hard in an advanced country to evade the bureaucracy that gathers the data of ordinary life and compiles the records and statistics of the people. And once you are in the machine, you can be found.

And you certainly will be in it if you've bought a house. Electricity, gas, water, postal, electoral, taxation systems, and plenty of other systems I can't even think of at the moment will all have you documented. And there you are, waiting to be billed — or found and shot. Unless you take adequate precautions.

'Who owns the house, Olga? Who bought it?'

'Oh, you know. One of our trading companies, I believe.'

'Not you personally?'

'No,' she said, shaking her head. 'I must keep a low profile.'

That was something, I supposed. Better than nothing. But not much of a shield. Apart from anything else, diligent researchers with nothing else to do, and eager to develop and exhibit their expertise with computers, could get through or around that. Eventually. The trading company that bought the house could even be on a list known to be associated with the Podolskys.

Why, oh why, hadn't Leon put his foot down and said no to buying the damned place? They could just have leased or rented it, although that too would have required plenty of formal records of occupancy to be established and kept.

Seeing where my thoughts were taking me, Olga said, 'Leon was against buying the house, but I insisted on it. This was where I wanted to be.'

So there was your answer, I thought with a wry smile. Olga could be denied nothing — by any of us!

With a sigh, I moved on and asked again if she was aware of anything happening lately, anything that might be a threat.

'Nothing threatening, Frank. Nothing like that.'

'Like something else?'

'Just a few little things that seemed unusual, curious, but nothing important.'

'Like what?'

'Oh, you know!'

But I didn't. That was the trouble. I knew next to nothing about either the local scene or the big picture.

I pressed on.

'You need to tell me, Olga. Tell me anything that has caught your eye. It might mean more to me than it does to you.'

She told me of builders and tradesmen calling at the door, wanting to know if she needed any work done now she was living here. A man had come to offer his services as a gardener. There had been fliers put in the letter box advertising the benefits of installing heat pumps to supply warmth and hot water. The usual, you might say. And truly nothing out of the ordinary.

'Well, I don't want to worry you unnecessarily, Olga. And I realise how important your work is, and how determined you are to live as normal a life as possible, but I feel we need to take some precautions. Your brother feels the same way. That's why I'm here.'

'Oh, Leon! He worries so much,' she said with an affectionate smile.

'Perhaps he does at times, but I believe he's right about this. Times have changed. The situation in Ukraine means that things are more difficult everywhere now, especially for people of Russian origin who don't support the Kremlin, which Leon doesn't. So you need to take greater care, like so many other people around Europe.'

I didn't add that Olga was exceptionally vulnerable because of her role in the family business. There was no need. She knew that. Hit her, and Leon would probably struggle to hold his financial structure together. Wreck that, and his rivals and the Kremlin would have a lot less to worry about from the Podolsky family.

'What do you suggest, Frank?'

'Although I don't want to risk drawing attention to the house, I think we should make some plans and install a few defences. My focus at present is on the short term. Longer term, we'll have to think again.'

'Like at The Chesters, Frank?'

'Something like that.'

The first job Leon had given me at that old house in Northumberland was to check and improve physical security.

I'd done a pretty good job of setting up perimeter fencing, and security sensors and lighting, but the bad guys had come mob-handed and overwhelmed the defences. Without a standing army in place, they couldn't have been stopped. I would just have to hope that history didn't repeat itself.

'The fence around the boundary of the property is very flimsy,' I said. 'If we can find men capable of doing the work, we need to strengthen and replace it.'

'That won't be a problem,' Olga assured me.

'No?'

'Leon will send a construction crew, if necessary.'

'That would be good. I'm not suggesting a high fence, or one made of steel mesh. Nothing like that. This isn't an industrial estate. What we need here is an unobtrusive but strong low fence, no more than a metre high. Made of solid timber beams, supported by heavy-duty timber posts concreted into the ground. Plus a strong, reinforced gate. That would prevent just about anything but a main battle tank crashing through.'

'OK, Frank. What else?' she asked, making a note.

'The usual electronic security systems — sensors, cameras, alarms, etc.'

I stopped. Olga was frowning.

'What?'

'I'm not sure I would like that, Frank.'

I knew why. She hadn't moved to the countryside to live like the Podolskys had to do in a big city. She wanted to hear birds sing and the wind blow. Probably see dark skies, as well.

'You live alone, Olga,' I said gently. 'Nobody to warn you of approaching danger. I can be here for a few weeks, but not for ever.'

Her face set hard. Her mind was made up. 'I will manage,' she said.

'OK,' I said. 'It's your call. If you really don't want technology out there in your garden, how about a big dog — preferably two big dogs?'

Her face lit up with a smile now. 'I would like that, Frank,' she admitted.

Thank God for that! I thought. At least it was something.

'But for now, we should put in detectors to warn of intruders,' I said firmly.

Reluctantly, she conceded the point. She knew it would take time to find and train appropriate dogs.

I moved on to other things that I thought it would be at least useful to consider. Always, though, I was mindful of Olga's sensitivities. She didn't want to live in a fortress, surrounded by armed guards. That was why she was here, after all, and not in Prague. So anything I suggested had to be proportionate.

How sustainable living here alone would be for her in the longer term was another matter altogether, but that wasn't one for me. There was nothing I could do about it. I was even more helpless than Leon when it came to that.

One thing I was sure about was that she needed a safe space she could retreat to if things ever did turn bad. A panic room, in other words, although I didn't use that term. No point introducing the word *panic* into the conversation.

The obvious place for such a facility was the basement. In fact, the whole of the stone basement could be turned into a formidable refuge, the equivalent of the medieval castle keep or the bastle, the fortified farmhouse, that Northumbrians used to withdraw to when the Scots came raiding across the border.

'If we can get a work crew in,' I said, 'we can have a heavy-duty door installed. It might not stop invaders permanently, but it would hold them up and allow you time to summon help.'

'Yes,' she said thoughtfully. 'There is a good door already, but I should establish a communication system that will work from there.'

'Good. Longer term, I would suggest constructing a secret way of escape from the basement, as well.'

'Oh?'

'A tunnel, perhaps.'

'Yes! That would be better than remaining shut up down there.'

'Finally, Olga, I would also suggest that you prepare an emergency way of closing down and perhaps destroying your IT systems.

'Have an emergency button that, once pressed, would mean intruders could never access your systems or your data. You would need to be able to do that from wherever you are at the time. Perhaps by using your phone?'

She nodded. 'I can do that, as well. It is simple.'

We left it there for the moment. We had covered a lot of ground, and I didn't want to fret over what couldn't be done.

CHAPTER TWENTY-EIGHT

Zeman's HQ, Prague

That first night in Prague, Kravertz struggled to get any sleep. Initially, Smith was the problem. It was a long time since Kravertz had shared a bedroom with someone who snored, and Smith did that, all right. Even waking Smith up a couple of times did no good. As soon as he returned to sleep, the snoring began again. Not for the first time, Kravertz wondered if he might have been better off if he'd come alone.

There were plenty of things on his mind, as well, troubling things. Smith had prompted them with his concerns and questions. Kravertz wasn't bothered that only Zeman amongst the Czechs seemed to speak English. He couldn't give a damn what they discussed in their own language. What bothered him was that they were a rough bunch, and not the smooth operators he had expected, given Manny's assurances. These were not financial or high-tech crime exponents; they were criminal muscle, pure and simple. And that made him wonder about their connection to Manny, and the organisation.

Then again, what did he know of the Brotherhood? The only contact he had ever had was with, or through, Manny.

And Jed Smith had played a useful part in reminding him of that fact. Maybe he should have been more careful all along, instead of trusting Manny to do the right thing and protect and further his interests.

Given how little he knew about where the money to set up KOSC had come from, that was not a thought to encourage a good night's sleep, even if he hadn't been sharing the room with a snorer.

CHAPTER TWENTY-NINE

Kámen

I'll say this for Olga. Dreamy she might be, but once she had decided something should be done, she could move as fast as any other member of the Podolsky family. Within a couple of days, a construction crew arrived, and so did wagons bringing timber, wire, cement, gravel and all the other materials I had specified. Work began.

The paling fence around the perimeter of the property was in poor condition, and non-existent now in places, but I wanted it rebuilt rather than removed. It was a traditional screen that people in the village were accustomed to seeing, and to the extent it was possible, I wanted to avoid them getting agitated about something unusual going on here.

At the same time as the flimsy paling fence was being restored, the crew began building the heavy-duty barrier I had discussed with Olga a metre inside the fence. This consisted of heavy timber beams supported by sturdy timber posts set deep in the ground in beds of concrete. It was only a couple of feet high but it was unobtrusive, and would stop any vehicle that wasn't something like a bulldozer.

The foreman in charge of the construction crew, Vladimir, seemed a good guy. Nothing was a problem to him, and we got on well together from the start. Once work was under way on the perimeter defences, he started thinking about the tunnel I was considering and began drilling holes to assess the nature of the ground around the house. I left him to it and went to pursue another thought I'd had.

* * *

'Olga, you use the village shops, don't you?'

'Of course,' she said, looking up from her computer screen. 'Sometimes,' she added. 'Why do you ask?'

'Do you talk to the people working there? Perhaps one in particular?'

'The older woman in the shop where I buy bread,' she said with a shrug. 'She is nice to me. What are you thinking, Frank?'

'I'm thinking it would be a good idea to tell her something about the work going on here. People in the village will notice, and wonder about it. To stop them guessing and speculating, and becoming obsessed with it, why not let the woman in the shop know you're just getting some repairs done? And renovating the house.

'She'll pass that on, and people will understand. They'll all know what the property is like. It must have been derelict for years until you took it on.'

'Yes. That is a good idea. I will go there this morning.'

* * *

That was another thing taken care of. What else was there for me to do? Plenty. But I needed to do some thinking, as well. One thing I kept in mind was that notwithstanding Olga's customary relaxed manner, she really was in danger. Hiding away in the Czech countryside might make her feel more safe and secure than she would be in Prague, but she wasn't. She could still be found by people being paid to look for her.

Still, Leon had brought me in not as a permanent bodyguard, but because there was a short-term crisis that he believed would peak in a few weeks. So there was no point dwelling on the long term. I needed to focus on the immediate future. That meant the escape tunnel couldn't be a top priority, although I didn't want it kicked into the long grass, either. It was just more of a long-term project.

For now, I focused on perimeter defence, and I knew what more I wanted for that. I put in a call to Leon, asking him to procure some essentials for me: sensors, lights, cameras, and warning gadgets. Essentially, it was the same sort of stuff that I had installed at Chesters, as well as elsewhere. Olga might not like some of it. So I would avoid the big stuff and be careful about what I installed.

'Tomorrow, Frank,' Leon assured me. 'You will have it all first thing in the morning. We will bring it overnight.'

'Is that your "first thing", Leon, or mine?'

He laughed. 'Perhaps by four it will be there. Maybe five if the courier is a slow driver.'

'Good thing I asked, then. I'll make sure I'm up and ready for an early start.'

Leon had never kept what might be called normal hours. Not since I had known him, anyway. The day was twenty-four hours long, his business and other interests were global, and it didn't matter to him what hour of the day things got done. Or when he slept, for that matter. He did his sleeping when there was time for it, and when the need for it could no longer be put off.

I assumed it was a way of living he had become used to during his time in the military. Special forces in anyone's army were not like ordinary footsloggers. Sometimes I wondered if he was any different when he visited his wife and children in Switzerland. I hoped he was, but without much confidence.

'How are things there, in Kámen, Frank?'

'All right, I think. Olga seems well, and much the same as usual. The men you sent are working on the fence and barrier, as well as on other things. And I'm still exploring the possibilities.'

'Good. No sign of trouble?'

102

'No, nothing. But I'm not ruling it out. I'm very aware of how vulnerable Olga is here, especially after what happened at the airport.'

'More so than ever, Frank. What she is doing now is very important.'

Important to whom, I wondered? But the conversation ended soon afterwards, leaving me none the wiser. The way things were, I also wondered if I should be asking for a pay rise, or danger money. My standard daily charge didn't seem to cover what was afoot here, or what was required of me.

CHAPTER THIRTY

A day or so later, in the evening, Jimmy Mack phoned again.

'What's up, Jim?'

I knew there had to be something. It's a very rare thing to get a phone call from Jimmy when I'm away. He has my number, for emergencies, but he's hardly ever used it.

'I thought you should know there's been a young feller here, looking for you. Jamie . . . something, he's called. It's the same one Bill Peart mentioned when he was here. He said he's met you, and he was disappointed when I told him you were away working. In fact, he looked a bit lost, as if he didn't know what to do next.'

I sighed. Whatever the problem, I still doubted there was anything I could do about it.

'It would have been Jamie Burke, Jim. He's in trouble, and probably just wanted a friendly shoulder to cry on.'

'Well, I don't know what the problem is, but he seemed a nice enough feller to me.'

'He didn't tell you what it was about?'

'No, nothing.'

I didn't tell Jimmy anything either. No point. There was nothing he could do. Even less than I could.

'What should I tell him if he comes back?'

'Refer him to Bill Peart. And call Bill yourself, if you like. It's a police matter, and Bill knows all about it. In fact, he's supposed to be helping Jamie.'

'Right. That's what I'll do, then.'

* * *

'Problems?' Olga asked sympathetically, having overheard the discussion.

I shook my head. 'Not really. Not for me, anyway. It was just my neighbour letting me know that someone wanting my help was looking for me. But there's nothing I can do for him.'

'You're always helping people, aren't you, Frank?'

'Only if I can't avoid it,' I told her with a grin.

'Oh, no! I don't believe that. But you really can't help this poor man?'

I shook my head. 'Unfortunately, I don't think anyone can, apart from the police. He'll have to go to them.'

* * *

We left it there and got on with our evening meal. Afterwards, Olga had some things she wanted to do, and I left her to them and went for a walk around the village. We both needed some personal time, just as Vladimir and his men did. They had stopped work for the day and were busy playing a game of cards in one of the big, vacant rooms.

Inevitably, my thoughts took me back to the conversation with Jimmy Mack. I did wonder what Jamie Burke had wanted. Perhaps he really was just feeling lonely and needed to talk to someone. Or had something more happened? Perhaps it had, given that Bill Peart had been worried about not being able to contact him.

But I didn't know, and I didn't want to know. I was here. He was there. And that was all there was to it. I couldn't help Jamie. Bill Peart might be the only person who could, if he could find him.

Having reached that conclusion, I returned to the house, and to Olga. She was someone I hoped I would be able to help.

* * *

'You left your phone,' Olga said. 'And while you were out, there was another incoming call for you.'

'Oh? Did you answer it?'

'Of course not.'

I picked up the phone and glanced at it. Then I wished I hadn't.

CHAPTER THIRTY-ONE

Now it was Henry Bolckow trying to contact me, and wanting me to call him back. I knew what it would be about. I was getting very tired of hearing the name "Jamie Burke". More of this, and I'd have to change my phone number.

Still, I couldn't ignore Henry. I couldn't afford to do that. He might start ignoring urgent calls from me.

'Henry. I got your message. What's up?'

'I'm worried about Jamie. I haven't been able to get him on the phone, and he hasn't called me for a few days. I wondered if you knew anything that might explain it.'

I sighed. Someone else worried about the man in the spotlight. How many was that now, not counting me?

'A few days, you say, Henry? Would you normally expect to hear from him that often?'

'Yes.'

I waited, but he didn't say anything more. I wondered if he was taking time out to light another of his infernal cigarettes. A bout of coughing told me that was exactly what he'd been doing.

I gave it a few moments for the coughing to die down. Then I said, 'I'm away, working, right now, Henry. I'm abroad. There's nothing I can tell you about Jamie's current situation, I'm afraid. You'll be more up to date than me.'

'You're abroad?'

'Mmm.'

A significant pause suggested he didn't like that idea.

'Far abroad?'

'Central Europe.'

'Not too far, then.'

Meaning that I could easily return, if I wanted to. In Henry's opinion.

'Look, Henry. I've signed up to do a job here for some-one important to me. I'll be away a while.'

'It's always the same,' he grumbled.

He didn't sound happy about it, about me not being available when he wanted me to be. I felt like telling him more clearly how it was, and trying to put him straight. But I desisted.

'All I can tell you, Henry, is that I met Jamie about a week ago, as I told you I would. We had a good, long chat. And I liked him.

'He told me about his situation, and I was impressed by what he's doing. He's a good guy. I'm very sorry for him. I really am. I just wish there was something I could do to help him, but there isn't. And that's what I told him.'

'He said.'

'Oh? So you've spoken to him since then?'

'Yeah. He's an old pal of mine, a good pal.'

'Well, he's just going to have to rely on the police, and perhaps go back into Witness Protection.'

'They're no good,' Henry said firmly. 'He won't do that.'

'Well, he'll be on his own, if he doesn't.'

'There must be something you can do!'

'Like what? You tell me, Henry.'

He didn't, of course. He couldn't. Of course he couldn't. What could any one man do?

Relenting, trying to soften the pill, I said, 'What you could do meanwhile, Henry, is some research on KOSC. Jamie's in trouble because of them, or the guy who owns the company. See what you can find out about them, and get back to me. Maybe there'll be something we can use to help Jamie.'

'And you'll pay me for it?'

I grinned. Attaboy! Henry was recovering.

'Me pay you, Henry? I thought you said Jamie was a pal?'

'Oh, all right,' he said.

Then he ended the call.

CHAPTER THIRTY-TWO

I left the work going on with the fences and walked around the property, and then a bit further afield, trying to look at it as a potential attacker might do. It was an experience that didn't reassure me.

What we were definitely not doing was building an impregnable fortress. We were just trying to impede a potential attacker and slow him down, as well as giving early warning of his presence. No way could we actually stop him, not for long anyway. And if an attack was made by a determined, experienced, ruthless team, the delay might not be for very long at all.

All this added up to one thing, given that Olga refused to move to somewhere safer. She needed an exit strategy, for use when — not if — necessary.

There needed to be stages to it. First, as we'd already discussed, she had to be able to permanently disable the computer system at a stroke, or push of a button. It didn't matter about the machines themselves. She just needed to ensure they wouldn't work anymore, and their data couldn't be accessed. If they just became scrap, so what? They could easily be replaced and work resumed elsewhere.

As it happened, I was quite sure anyway that backups already existed, of both data and actual computer set-ups. I'd seen that to be the case in the past, and I knew it wouldn't be any different now. No way could the Podolskys afford to allow all their systems and data to reside in only one IT centre.

Given time, the basement could be strengthened into a panic room, but until that had been done, Olga needed to keep an emergency pack close at hand. She also needed an escape route — perhaps more than one — from the house, and from Kámen itself. Long term, a tunnel could provide a way out of the house, but it was going to take time to build one. We needed to have an exit plan ready for imminent use.

I looked first at how best to get out of Kámen in a hurry. How to get out of the house was something I put to one side for the moment.

Assuming it could be reached, the SUV I had arrived in would make a perfectly good escape vehicle. But we needed to keep it out of sight, hidden, until that moment arrived. Until then, Olga's own little car would be enough for us to get about locally. That lived on the track outside the house, or in the big shed nearby, and it could stay there.

It was time for me to talk to Olga again.

* * *

'I don't want to alarm you, Olga, but we need to talk again about an emergency exit strategy, in case things go wrong for you.'

'You're so serious, Frank!' she said with a smile.

'After my experience at the airport, and after talking to Leon and hearing his concerns, damned right I'm serious! We must think about what could happen, and plan how to deal with it.

'If something does occur, we don't want to find ourselves wondering only then what to do about it, and wasting valuable time. We'll need to be up and out as fast as possible — however much you like it here.'

'I know,' she said with a sigh. 'You are quite right, Frank. I was only teasing. What do you have in mind? And what do you want me to do?'

I went through it again with her, feeling like an old-fashioned schoolteacher dealing with an errant child.

After hearing me out, she said, 'I have already set up an automatic decommissioning plan for our systems here.'

'Oh?' I said with surprise. 'That's good. How will it work?'

'One of two ways. If I am here, in the basement, I can pull down the red lever near the door. That is the simplest and most direct method.'

I looked over to the door and noted the red lever. She must have had Vladimir install it. I thought how primitive, old-fashioned even, it looked. It was surprising she had even considered a manual lever, given the electronic world she inhabited.

'You're sure that would work?'

'Oh, yes. It would be very effective, and nothing can go wrong with such a simple thing. It would cut the supply of energy to the brain, if I can put it like that, and with its last breath the brain would say *Go!* to the destruction process.'

I shook my head. I didn't care for the overly simplistic explanation, but she was trying to make it easy for me to understand.

'OK. I accept what you're saying. But what if you're nowhere near that red handle? In bed, say? Or out in the garden, or the village? What then?'

'Then the other method would come into play. I send the main computer a simple code from my phone, laptop or any other device, and the destruction process would begin immediately.'

'Could it be stopped?'

She shook her head.

'Not even if power is cut to the house?'

'The brain has its own back-up power supply, a built-in battery, which is not on-site and couldn't be found at all quickly. Besides, the entire process would be very, very fast

112

and immediate. There would be no time for anyone to do anything about it, even if they knew how to.'

'Which they don't, and won't.'

She nodded.

So that seemed to be that, all possibilities covered. Sadly, though, it seemed to mean that an attack team would be best advised to focus on taking out Olga herself. That might be easier than taking over the computer.

* * *

'The other thing you mentioned,' Olga said with a frown, 'a garage for your car? I don't know where there is one.'

'Talk to the woman in the shop where you go for bread. Ask her.'

'You think she will know somewhere?'

'She'll know,' I said confidently. 'Tell her you will pay good money to rent garage space.'

'Why would I say I want it?'

'Because you don't expect to be using the vehicle much in the near future, but you don't want to sell it. You just want to keep it out of the weather. She will understand that.'

'Yes, I think you are right.' Still frowning, she added, 'But is she likely to know somewhere?'

'Yes.'

'Oh?'

'Trust me, Olga.'

She gazed wonderingly at me, as if doubting my assurance.

'There is an empty garage, a big shed at least, on land at the back of her own property. That would be perfect. And she is a businesswoman. She will seize the opportunity to make a little extra money when it appears.'

Olga smiled at last. 'Clever Frank! Once again, you have thought of everything.'

I didn't know about that, but I was flattered to hear that she thought so.

CHAPTER THIRTY-THREE

Almost all that could be done had been done, or was getting done. But it still wasn't enough. I knew that, felt that with the whole of my being, and it worried me greatly. Olga was pretty much a sitting duck here, and I had just about reached the limit of what I could do for her.

She should be somewhere else, somewhere safer, somewhere more like a fortress. She didn't see it like that, of course. I wasn't sure her brother did either, not really. They were both battle-hardened against adversity and used to living with risk.

What worried me particularly was that I was only one man. Ideally, Olga should have had a team of close protection officers with her. Then, allowance could have been made for 24/7 cover, rest, sickness, injuries, and anything else that might interfere with her protective screen.

But Olga would never accept such a level of security. I knew that even without asking her. She had made it clear that she wanted as normal a life as possible, and that didn't include having a big bunch of tough men living alongside her at all times. Or tough women, either. She wanted to be able to hear the birds and smell the flowers.

So there was just me. For now, at least, we had Vladimir and the construction crew with us. There was some comfort in that. They were a rugged bunch and I was glad they were around. I would just have to talk again to Leon about the longer-term situation.

Even so, I decided to have another go at Olga about moving house, and going where there could be more protection provided for her. Leon's house in Prague would be ideal in that respect, but surely somewhere else could be found for her, if that didn't suit?

Olga wouldn't hear of it.

'Dear Frank, I know you have my best interests at heart, and I do appreciate it, but the answer is still no. This is my home. Here, I am free. No guards. No barbed wire. I live as I please. You are providing me with enough protection, Frank. I am satisfied.'

So that was that. I hadn't really expected her to say anything else. I accepted defeat, smiled as graciously as I could manage and took myself off to see how work was progressing outside.

* * *

Something else that had been bothering me ever since I arrived was that Olga's computer room was nothing like the Podolsky IT centre at Chesters, or the one at Samphire Batts on the north shore of the Tees. There were no other people present, for one thing. Only Olga. Here, she was a one-man band.

Nor was there anything like as many screen displays and chattering printers as I remembered, particularly from my visits to Samphire Batts. It had been a bit of a mad house there, with machines humming and clattering away day and night, technicians attending them devotedly and analysts rushing around urgently with screeds of printout. And Olga presiding over it all in her own calm, inimitable style. This house was nothing like that.

Yet surely the Podolskys' global financial business and their online advisory service were still running? Their subscribers and all the data feeds and everything else couldn't have been scrapped and abandoned. That financial business service was a key cornerstone of Leon's empire. Without it, he wouldn't be a pauper, but he would be diminished financially, and in other ways too. Surely it hadn't all gone?

No, of course not! The core IT centre had to be elsewhere, I decided. Somewhere secret, and safe. Perhaps Switzerland, alongside so many other powerful and secretive players in the world's financial markets. That would make sense.

Especially so given that Switzerland had long been a tacit truce zone for the world's warring factions, a territory where fortunes and loved ones could be deposited and housed with confidence that they would be safe. Lots of people needed such a place, the likes of Putin as much as the Podolskys. Even Hitler's Nazis had known that. It was in no one's interest to break the unwritten rules.

What I had to wonder, though, was in that case what was Olga doing here, working alone in splendid isolation. She seemed busy enough. If she was still engaged with the main business, this really was distance working par excellence.

* * *

Vladimir came to tell me they had completed work on the outer fence and the inner barrier, and were almost ready to begin tunnelling, starting from the house.

'You can handle that?' I asked him. 'We don't need to bring in specialists?'

He grinned. 'We are specialists! What do you think soldiers in the army do?'

'Shoot guns, perhaps?'

'Sometimes,' he conceded, 'but mostly, especially in the construction division, we used to dig tunnels and trenches. It is why Leon wanted us. Now we do that for him.'

He laughed uproariously and went away, possibly to start digging the tunnel, leaving me chuckling and shaking my head. I might have known Leon would have made good use of his connections and personal experience when recruiting a construction team. Whichever army they had been in, though, Russia's or Ukraine's, I knew these were men whose hearts would be with Ukraine. They were Leon's sort of people, through and through.

CHAPTER THIRTY-FOUR

'What are you working on here, Olga? It's not Leonomics, is it? When I visited your place on Teesside there must have been at least a dozen people working there at all times. Here, there's just you.'

'That's right, Frank,' she said with a smile. 'Just me. That's how I like it.'

'So?'

'Well, my role is different now. Leonomics looks after itself most of the time. I wouldn't say the business is routine, but it is well established, and the managers know what they are doing.'

'And they are located elsewhere, obviously?'

'Of course. They are at arm's length, somewhere safe. Sadly, it has to be like that, because rivals and enemies made it impossible for us to function in the open.

'I keep an overall eye on things. Otherwise, I undertake special projects, things that interest me.'

That was more or less what I had thought. What she hadn't said was anything about those special projects. I still wondered what she did all day, and every day.

We were having lunch together. Potato soup with small *knedliky* dumplings. It was a simple, traditional meal prepared by Olga. I liked it a lot.

'So?' I said, trying again. 'What about right now? I ask only because it might impact on what I'm doing. It would help me to know what, or who, we are up against.'

She took her time responding.

'How much do you know, Frank? How much has Leon told you?'

'Not a lot, to be honest.'

'No. He wouldn't.'

It was irritating to have been kept in the dark, but realistically, Podolsky business affairs were no business of mine. Friendship only went so far.

Besides, Leon seemed to run a sort of cell system, even with his family, based on the need-to-know principle. It was the Russian tradition, I suppose. How he'd been brought up, and spent his formative years.

'But you are our friend, Frank,' Olga said carefully. 'Our very good friend. And you are here with us right now. So I believe you should be told something.'

'Thank you, Olga,' I said with a smile. 'That's exactly how I feel.'

'Leon has agreed that we will do some urgent work for the British Admiralty, and at the moment I am spending much time working on that project. We have a contract with them.'

'Oh? Well, Leon did say something about that — working with the Admiralty. But he didn't tell me you were involved. He just said the work was in the North Sea, where I met him aboard a trawler recently. But Kámen is a very long way from the North Sea — or from any sea.'

Olga smiled and nodded agreement.

'Even so, Frank, this inland country long had admirals.'

'For the river boats?' I suggested with a chuckle.

'Oh, no! They used to be based in Verona, I believe, or perhaps Trieste,' she said with a sunny smile. 'That was in the days when this little country was part of a very big state that had armies, navies and everything else it was possible to have.'

119

'That right? So the Habsburg Empire, or Austria-Hungary, had everything but an air force?'

'Yes.'

'I wonder what happened to all the Czech admirals? Perhaps they emigrated to America?'

'Or just came home, and grew potatoes?' she suggested, laughing.

'OK, Olga. But I still don't know much about what you are doing for the British Admiralty.'

'It is very simple. We have a specialist under-sea monitoring capability, which we developed with the Israelis in the Red Sea and Persian Gulf. The Admiralty asked us to work with them on checking the security of oil and gas pipelines and other connectors on the seabed, especially those crossing from Norway to Great Britain.

'There is a growing concern that they are very vulnerable to attack, and Leon was asked to monitor the situation in a sector off the coast of North East England.'

'Where I live,' I pointed out.

'Yes, of course. Risky Point, isn't it?'

I was thinking that began to explain what Leon had been doing on my patch when he summoned my presence so indecorously.

'I met him there recently,' I said slowly, 'but on a fishing trawler, not some sort of research vessel.'

'We have several such ships, Frank. They are not what they seem. It is necessary sometimes to be in disguise. But I can assure you that all of them have very special capabilities.'

Spy ships, then. Capable of covert operations. Like the traditional Russian trawlers.

I shook my head. The sheer range of Podolsky operations continued to amaze me. I had to wonder what had made Leon acquire such ships in the first place — not that I could ask, or that he would tell me. I would just get some cock-and-bull story if I did ask.

'But you are here, Olga. Don't you like the sea? Do you get seasick?'

She laughed softly. 'It is true that I have no love for the ocean. I do my best to avoid visiting it. But what I do in relation to our project in the North Sea, I can do from here, or anywhere else, perfectly well.'

'Oh? And what might that be?'

'I am spending much time operating drones in the sector for which we have responsibility.'

'You can do that from here?'

'Of course. Military drones in places like Iraq and Afghanistan have long been flown from bases as far away as California. The North Sea, from here, is nothing like that distance. Also, our IT centre on Teesside acts as a relay station for my instructions, as well as a launch pad and maintenance base for the drones.'

Amazing. I could scarcely believe it.

'What do the drones do? Don't tell me they can go underwater?'

'Of course they can, and they do. They skim along the pipelines, feeding back information to the computers, and the technicians, so that we can look for signs of problems, or disturbance.'

'It sounds like fantasy, or science fiction, to me, Olga. I had no idea such technology was available.'

She smiled and took pity on me. 'How could you know, Frank? You are not in this business. But such drones have been used in the oil industry for many years.'

Kindly done, but I was put in my place. I was an utter ignoramus, it seemed.

CHAPTER THIRTY-FIVE

Olga must have spoken to Leon after my conversation with her, as that afternoon the man himself arrived in Kámen, unannounced, travelling in a Skoda SUV with only a driver as company. I opened the gate for them. They parked just inside and Leon got out.

'*Dobrý den*, Frank!' Good day.

'Leon! This is a surprise.'

We shook hands and he gave me a big grin.

'I thought I should tell you more about what is happening, Frank. I didn't want you distracting Olga anymore,' he added cheerfully.

'I see. Well, I appreciate the visit.'

'How are things going?' he asked, turning on his heel to look at what was going on.

Vladimir waved, and Leon waved back. Old friends.

'Have you got everything you need?' Leon asked me.

'For the moment, thanks. And Vladimir and his men are doing really well.'

'Good. Let's go inside. I will say hello to Olga, and then you and I can talk more about what is going on. Olga said she told you some of it?'

122

I nodded. 'But I need to know more, Leon. I don't want to be guessing all the time.'

'OK. I will tell you.'

* * *

'It's like this,' Leon said when we got settled in the kitchen with coffee. 'The work with the Admiralty is ongoing, but one part of it is very urgent.

'It's November twenty-third now,' he said, glancing at his watch for confirmation. 'Intelligence sources have picked up that December sixteenth, which is less than four weeks away, is the date for a major terrorist incident involving sub-sea infrastructure off the coast of North East England.'

'Intelligence sources?'

'British. The Admiralty have access to them, or have been warned by them.'

I nodded.

'And that's it,' Leon added. 'That is all that is really known. All the rest is guesswork. But it is enough to have created panic in London.'

It sounded to me as if GCHQ had picked up something, a fragment of something, through their constant monitoring of the world's communications traffic. Not much, obviously, but enough for people in high places to get excited.

'And that's why the Admiralty approached you?'

Leon nodded. 'I said we would be glad to help, and here we are.'

'And you really don't know what you're looking for?'

'The assumption is that it's an attempt to sabotage a pipeline, either oil or gas. That would cut energy supplies to the UK, cause much pollution and generate a lot of unfavourable headlines in the world's media. How inadequate the government is at protecting the British people, for example.'

He was right about that, I thought. It was how the media worked.

'Who's doing it, do you think? Best guess?'

123

Leon pursed his lips and frowned before he replied. 'I have to tell you no one knows at this stage. It could be a state actor, or someone acting for them, in which case I would put money on Russia, for obvious reasons. Perhaps Iran. Maybe China, though that's less likely. Or it could be one of the usual Islamist terrorist organisations.'

'Or?' I said, when I saw him hesitate, as if he hadn't finished.

'Or it could be corporate business interests, hoping to somehow make a lot of money out of something like this.'

'How could that work?'

'Simple. Consider oil for a moment. At any given moment in time, the world's oceans are full of tankers carrying oil. There were nearly ten thousand of them in 2021. Some are state-owned or oil-company-owned. But three-quarters of them are independently owned.

'Many of the independents are contracted, for periods of months or years, but plenty are not. They can just sail the seven seas, like a big storage tank, waiting for the price to be right before they decide who gets their oil.'

'And there are big profits in this business, presumably?'

'There can be. It depends on all sorts of things, of course, but one of the very big tankers can generate a daily profit of as much as $100,000.'

'Phew!' I whistled with surprise. 'Time your offload right, and make a killing, eh?'

Leon nodded. 'And there are owners who would do a lot to create a favourable market for their oil.'

'By fair means or foul?'

'That's right.'

I was struggling to get my head around it all. One thing was pretty clear, though. Blowing up an oil pipeline could well create a lot of money for people who had a tanker of oil they were ready to step forward with to sell at a moment's notice, at an inflated price.

* * *

124

Something else that was clearer now was why Olga was particularly at risk for the next few weeks. Podolsky involvement must have leaked, and whoever was behind all this would do a lot to stop her interfering with their scheme, regardless of whether it was a state actor or a private corporation.

'The sixteenth of December, huh?' I said with a grimace. 'That's when there could be a very big bang, unless it can be stopped?'

Leon spread his arms with frustration. 'The intelligence isn't much to go on, but it's being taken very seriously by the experts in this field.'

He was right. It really wasn't much to go on, but it couldn't be ignored. Too much was at stake. The many unknowns would have to stay that way for the time being.

'Well, thanks for the briefing, Leon. I appreciate your coming here to tell me.'

'Oh, I didn't come only for that reason. I have things to discuss with Olga, as well.'

I nodded. I was sure he did.

Later, before he left, I asked him about Charles.

'He is the same. Still in a coma. Still being supported by machines. Nothing has changed.'

I grimaced, but at least he was no worse. That was something.

CHAPTER THIRTY-SIX

I had thought, and hoped, that the task I'd set him would get Henry off my back for a while. Getting him to research KOSC had been the best thing I could think of at the time he was on the phone to me. It didn't work, though, not for long anyway. He was back a few days later, when I was in a meeting with Olga.

'Henry! How are you?'

He mumbled and grumbled something conventional, which I didn't really catch. I didn't bother asking him to repeat it either. Henry doesn't do well, or cheerful. Usually he just does complaints and savage criticism.

'Has Jamie been in touch, Henry?'

'No.'

That was it. End of story. Then he launched into what was really on his mind.

'That KOSC are a piece of work. Did you know that?' he demanded.

'Not really. But from what I'd heard from Jamie it sounded likely. What have you got?'

'They're supposed to be an offshore company, but really they're part of an organised crime syndicate.'

'I didn't think Teesside was big enough to have one of them.'

'Oh, boy!' Henry spluttered with what sounded like indignation. 'You haven't heard much, have you? You need to get out more.'

I had to grin. Old Henry was pretty worked up about this, I could tell.

'Come on, then! What have you got? Aren't they an offshore company?'

'Well, to some extent they are. But, first, KOSC are just one arm of the syndicate, which is national and even international. They are, like, the local branch of a global monster, my sources tell me.'

'I see.'

'But they're pretty much free-standing. KOSC have operational independence. To an extent, they can do what they like. They just have a lot of back-up if they need it, and they pay money into a central kitty. A guy called Mannheim, based in Germany, is the European end of it.'

'I see,' I said again, starting to wonder how long a call this was going to be. Henry hadn't really got going yet.

'KOSC, itself, is supposed to be owned and managed by one man, although I don't know where his money came from. Neither do the National Crime Agency, actually, which is why this inquiry's going on. Anyway, he's a Yank called Daniel J. Kravertz, who comes from Cleveland.'

'He's a local, in other words?'

'Cleveland, Ohio,' Henry said impatiently.

'Oh, that one. A genuine Yank, then.'

'Well . . .'

I shook my head, raised eyeballs to the ceiling and willed Henry to get on with it.

'Venture capitalist, is he?'

'Very much so. But a crime boss, as well. He still likes to do the little stuff as well as the big stuff.'

'Like rigging boxing tournaments?'

'Yeah. Jamie got in with the wrong guy there. He was out of his depth from the start. But the big game for Kravertz is legitimate offshore activities, mostly decommissioning and dismantling oil rigs.

'There's a few Teesside companies into that, now the North Sea oilfields are running out of the black stuff. Sometimes the dismantling is being done by the same company that built the thing thirty or forty, or even more, years ago.

'Funny, isn't it,' he mused, 'how crime gangs tend to congregate around waste disposal, scrap metal collection, demolition sites? Always good pickings for them around rubbish, one way or another.'

Henry wasn't wrong. He had a good point. But I decided to cut him off in full flow. Otherwise, he could be on the phone all night.

'Sorry, Henry. I have to go. I've got a lot on at the moment. You're doing well with your enquiries, but I'll have to hear more another time. I'll get back to you.'

'OK,' he said dubiously.

'Hang on to what you're doing, Henry. And see if you can get more on the background to Jamie's problem.'

I ended the call and sat back with relief.

'Where were we?' I asked Olga.

'It never stops, does it?' she said sympathetically.

'Never. Just one damn thing after another.'

CHAPTER THIRTY-SEVEN

The way I was thinking was that I had more than enough to worry about without Henry trying to take me back to Jamie Burke's situation. I didn't need problems from home on top of the ones I had here.

Then things got even worse. Vladimir told me he and his men had to return to Prague. They were needed urgently there, apparently. An emergency. That eclipsed thoughts of Henry and Jamie Burke

I couldn't object. Vladimir and his men had done nearly everything here I had asked them to do, except build the tunnel. That had been started, but they needed more equipment to make further progress. They would bring that with them, Vladimir said, when they returned in a week or two to complete the job.

I thanked him, and watched with foreboding as they left. I don't mind admitting I wasn't pleased about it, but what could I do? For them, for Leon, we weren't the only game in town. Besides, there wasn't any sign of an active threat here to Olga at the moment. I was just insurance, in case something did happen.

But the presence of Vladimir and company had been an enormous reassurance and confidence booster that Olga and

I had now lost. In just a few days, they had achieved a great deal. Olga's safety was far from assured, but much had been done to make an attack on her more difficult, and to warn if one was imminent.

I didn't know what else I could do so long as the lady herself insisted on staying here in this remote and vulnerable place, with only me for protection. More than ever, I was acutely aware of being on my own, in a situation where a team was needed. I couldn't be constantly on guard, night and day. It wasn't only the immediate future that concerned me either. I could stay a little longer than agreed, if necessary, but not indefinitely. No way did I want to become a permanent night watchman. But what would happen after I left?

It was a big house, too. Far too big for one person. Or one normal person, I should say. I wouldn't have wanted to live there alone, as Olga had been doing for a year until my arrival. But that was down to her, and Olga was different, as I've already said many times.

Along with her special abilities went a special way of looking at things, and even just of living. Leon and the rest of the family had long accepted that, and it was what I had to do, too. There was no way any of us would or could want her to be any different. We didn't even try to make her change, not seriously.

Even so, the departure of Vladimir and his men left me very uneasy that first evening after they had gone. The house seemed empty. It was empty. It echoed. I didn't like that. It was as if we were rattling around in an empty shell. There could be things going on in different parts of it that we didn't even suspect. The fact that nothing bad had happened here since Day One of Olga's arrival a year ago didn't make me feel any better.

While there had been half a dozen of Leon's men with us, I had been able to relax. Always there had been someone on watch, someone to share the duty of constant vigilance. Now there was only little old me.

Before nightfall came I toured the property, checking to make sure everything was in order. There hadn't been time yet to find two suitable guard dogs and train them, never mind dig an emergency escape tunnel, but the alarms and sensors on the fences were set and working normally. The gates were closed and locked. The village was peaceful. Apart from the occasional vehicle passing through, and one or two people walking their dogs, there was nothing happening. All seemed well. Yet I still wasn't comfortable or satisfied.

We had a simple evening meal together that I helped Olga prepare. It involved noodles and eggs, together with a salad and slices of the traditional dense rye bread that was so common here and in other parts of central and eastern Europe. For myself, I would have preferred a crusty French baguette, but I kept quiet and reasoned that the spartan fare was probably good for me.

We talked. Not a lot, but enough to make it a pleasant and companionable evening. Olga told me a little more about her work and showed me a video, taken by a drone, of the seabed zone the Podolskys were monitoring. She was looking at pipelines for signs of interference, and there were a good many pipelines to examine. Some were to do with offshore wind farms. Others carried oil or gas long distances, even from as far away as Norway. Only three weeks to go now, as well. Like me, Olga had a big job to do for only one person.

* * *

Our bedrooms, Olga's and mine, were close together for security reasons. As her close protection officer, I wanted to be nearby in case of need, and that seemed to suit her as well.

They were simple rooms, a few paces apart along a dusty corridor lined with wooden floor and walls. The rooms were similarly clad in unadorned timber. Mine, I couldn't help thinking, was probably no different to when the carpenters finished building it and left, centuries ago.

It put me in mind of scenes remembered from childhood fairy tales. Appropriately, it had an attic window, a boarded wooden floor that creaked, a massive chest of drawers, a rocking chair, and a single bed with an ornate headboard depicting scenes that looked as if they were somewhere in the Slavonic world of endless forest.

Olga's room was much the same, plus lots of the kind of frills I remembered from her flat in Prague: bunches of dried wild flowers, old pictures of ancient people hay-making and skating on frozen ponds, timber churches with onion dome towers. Possibly Mother Russia. But more likely to be just Slav culture before or without borders. The world depicted by Mucha's "Slav Epic", that vast display of a people's progress over the millennia which I had once seen on display in Prague in the National Gallery's Collection of Modern Art.

'I don't want to worry you, Olga,' I said, as we parted at the end of the evening, 'but we must be more vigilant now that Vladimir and his men have left us. You must keep everything essential to you in a bag by your side. I will do the same. Then, if anything unfortunate happens, which seems unlikely at the moment, we can leave quickly and make our way to the car. Agreed?'

Olga smiled. 'Oh, yes! You have made everything perfectly clear, Frank. And I will be ready to do what we have planned, if the time ever comes when it is necessary.'

She refrained from reminding me that she had lived here alone, without problems, for a year until I arrived, and had managed perfectly well. I just hoped that her sanguine air was justified, even if her brother didn't think so.

And I refrained from reminding her that Leon believed this was a critical period, and that was why he had brought me on board for her protection. Things were different now. There could be people out there determined to thwart what the Podolskys were doing for the Admiralty. The next couple of weeks were going to be critical.

I also didn't tell Olga that Leon being so obviously worried was why I was so worried, too. I didn't want to alarm her. I just wanted to make sure she was aware of the situation, and what we might have to do if things went haywire. Feeling alarmed and on edge were conditions that could be left with me.

After that we went to our rooms, and our beds, Olga in her customary sunny way and me full of apprehension, knowing how unlikely it was that I would actually sleep that night. I was ready to get up and go at the slightest hint of danger, and I knew that would be how it would be for me from now on.

CHAPTER THIRTY-EIGHT

Nothing happened!

I stayed awake through the small hours, tensed and waiting, but not one thing out of the ordinary occurred. Eventually, light began to appear around the edges of the curtains. Soon afterwards I heard the first bird call of the day. Then, shortly after that, what passes for the dawn chorus in November started. And, finally, I went to sleep.

'Poor Frank,' Olga said with a sympathetic smile when I showed up at the breakfast table. 'Is jet lag still responsible for your late rising, or have you been working too hard since you came here?'

'Don't rub it in,' I said with a groan, finding a couple of hours of sleep had not been nearly enough.

'I am sorry to make a joke,' Olga said. 'I know how badly lack of sleep can affect a person.'

'Don't worry about it,' I said brusquely, not wanting her to feel sorry for me. I didn't need that. I had a job to do. Besides, insufficient sleep while on a job wasn't exactly a novelty for me.

'You've finished breakfast, I take it?' I added, seeing her empty plate and cup.

'Yes. I have. I must go now, and start my work, if you will excuse me?'

'Of course.'

'Can I leave you to make your own breakfast, Frank?'

Funny! I gave her a rueful grin.

'That's what I'm used to doing, Olga. I'm poor company at the breakfast table anyway. That's when I plan for the day ahead.'

All of which was perfectly true.

And perhaps Olga was like that herself. My distinct impression was that she didn't eat a lot for breakfast, or at any other time of day either, judging by the contents of fridge and cupboards.

I made do that morning with coffee and a chunk of fruit cake, and made a mental note to suggest a shopping expedition for groceries. One of us needed to do something about that. Then I went outside to make my rounds of the property.

* * *

I don't mind admitting that I was relieved we had come through the night without incident. An attack hadn't been likely, when you thought about it objectively in the broad light of day. Not just a few hours after Vladimir and his men had left, but the possibility of one had been there. What Leon had told me had convinced me of that. So I'd been plenty worried. Now, though, it was a new day, and there were things to be done.

I got busy checking the fences, and the alarms and sensors, once again. All was in order. What could be done had been done. The only thing remaining on the to-do list was the escape tunnel, but nothing more could be done about that until Vladimir returned.

* * *

135

Next, I went to have a word with Olga about shopping.

'Yes,' she readily agreed. 'You go, Frank, if you don't mind. I have no time, I am afraid.'

Just as I thought.

I went to the little shop in the village that I had visited with Olga once or twice. The woman who owned it also owned the garage where we had stationed the Skoda. So she knew who I was. It helped, as well, that she spoke a little English. Having my car in her garage was a business arrangement, of course, but sometimes an arrangement like that works well in other ways, too.

'A man was here this morning,' the woman told me, as I paid for a basket of things I'd picked up.

'I'm not surprised. Your shop is important to the village,' I assured her.

She considered my reply before saying, 'Yes. But he buy nothing. I not like him.'

That made me smile. I hadn't realised that customers had to be to the liking of the shopkeeper. It was a very long time since that had been true at home, if ever.

'So what did he want?' I asked.

'He ask about the car in my garage — is it my car?'

This stranger had eyes on my car. That caught my interest rather more. I'd been cramming groceries into bags as she spoke. But now I paused, considering the implications of her words. A customer who didn't come here to shop . . . What was I missing?

'Oh? Why did he want to know that?'

'Who knows?' she said with a shrug. 'He not tell me when I ask him. So I not like him, for that and for other reasons.'

'What did you say to him?'

'I tell him yes, it is my car. Do you want to buy? He not reply. He look at me for long time. Then he leave.'

'You did well.'

It might simply have been curiosity from the shop visitor. All the same, she had been disturbed and her story made me uneasy too.

'Was he a local man, someone from the village?'

She shook her head. 'Never have I seen him. And he not Czech.'

'Oh? German, perhaps?'

'Not German, no. He speaks Czech, but like your wife does.'

My wife. I smiled wryly at the suggestion. Was that what she thought? It seemed unlikely. She was just being polite, and unable with her limited English to find another term.

It didn't matter. What did was that the man spoke with a Russian accent. That didn't seem good at all.

'Strange,' I said, my mind spinning now with possibilities.

'I hope you not angry when I say car is mine?'

'Not at all,' I assured her with a smile. 'You did the right thing. You are on your own here, and you needed to get him out of the shop, a man like that. Anyway, the car's not for sale. I don't want to get rid of it.'

'Good,' she said, sounding and looking relieved to hear it.

There was quite a lot on my mind as I walked back up the hill with the groceries. None of it was good.

CHAPTER THIRTY-NINE

Zeman's HQ, Prague

Zeman burst into the room. 'We have found where the Russian woman is!' he announced excitedly, with a big grin on his face.

'About time,' Kravertz said gruffly. 'We're getting tired of hanging around here.'

'You are free to leave whenever you wish,' Zeman said, colder now, the smile disappearing. 'Remember, you need us more than we need you.'

'OK, OK! Let's not disagree. So where is she?'

'Come with us, and find out. We leave in a few minutes.' Kravertz glanced at Smith. 'You ready, Jed?'

'Whenever you are,' Smith assured him.

'So? It is good?' Zeman asked.

Kravertz nodded. 'Let's go!'

* * *

'How far is it, this place?' Kravertz asked.

'Not so far,' Zeman assured him. 'Maybe two hours we get there. Or three. No more.'

Kravertz nodded. Long enough. He wanted to get it done and get out. He'd had enough of all this hanging around, Zeman and his cronies, this whole damned country!

He couldn't understand why Manny had ordered him here. It was almost like a punishment. Well, perhaps that was what it was. Retribution for messing things up with Burke. Manny showing him who was boss.

Put like that, he could understand it. Almost. But it sure as hell was no way to treat the guy who had built up KOSC for him!

But here they were, travelling in three big vehicles across a country that bored the hell out of him. At least it wouldn't be long now.

'We get there soon,' Kravertz said with satisfaction. 'We deal with her. Then we get the hell out.'

'Not so fast, my friend!' Zeman said with a chuckle. 'It won't be as easy as that. You must have more patience.'

'Oh? Why is that?'

'One reason is that the Podolsky woman will be protected. She will have her own security detachment.'

'We have the men to overcome that problem, surely?' Kravertz said dismissively.

'Mmm,' Zeman agreed. 'But we must assess the situation before we attack. Surely you understand that?'

Kravertz shrugged. It sounded like Zeman wanted to minimise casualties, but he didn't care how many men Zeman lost.

'Also,' Zeman said patiently, 'we need to look for a buyer for the woman. That takes time. Potential buyers have to be contacted. Negotiations have to take place. The price agreed.'

'What the hell are you talking about?' Kravertz demanded. 'I'm not here to talk about selling the bloody woman. I'm here because Manny wants her dead!'

'Eventually,' Zeman said calmly. 'But, first, she is very valuable. She knows much about the Podolsky business that certain people will pay a lot to learn. We must give them the chance to bid for that knowledge.'

'Manny said nothing about that,' Kravertz snapped.

'Oh, Manny! He is not the only one,' Zeman said loftily. 'He's your boss, as well as mine!'

'He is one of my bosses, but he is not the only one.'

Zeman looked at him with a calculating expression and added, 'It is different for you, perhaps?'

'No,' Kravertz said.

But it was. The situation was not how he had believed it to be. Zeman had a different goal in mind to him. He needed to reassess, and recalibrate.

At the same time, he also knew he couldn't afford to alienate Zeman. Do that, and he and Jed might just as well go home right now, job undone. As Zeman had already said, they needed him more than he needed them.

CHAPTER FORTY

Kámen

Olga was engrossed with a couple of screens in the basement, but she glanced round as I arrived and gave me a smile.

'Leonomics business?' I asked, seeing sheets of data on the screen she was currently examining.

'Yes. I must keep on top of what is happening at the main data centre.'

'Remote working, then?'

She nodded. Then she got up and moved to another bank of screens. 'This might interest you, Frank, now that Leon has spoken to you.'

I moved across to join her. What we were looking at was an overhead shot of a ship in dock. It was surrounded by cranes and small boats. Lots of activity was going on all around the ship, as well as on it.

'What's happening?' I asked, peering at the screen. 'They're loading something — cable reels?'

'Yes. The cable will connect a new wind farm in the North Sea to the UK mainland.'

'And you're keeping an eye on it?'

'As well as many other things,' she said with a shrug. 'Mostly, I look at pipelines.'

'Is this live coverage?'

'No. It is from early this morning. The last stage of the project.'

'A strange time of year for it. Usually, I would have thought, this kind of work will be finished by now, before the winter storms come in.'

'It's running late,' she said with a shrug.

I straightened up and pulled away.

'Olga, I don't like to worry you, but we need to talk. It's possible that the people looking for you have found us.'

She wheeled round and stared at me.

'I've just come back from the shop in the village. The woman there told me a man she didn't know asked if the car in her garage was hers. She didn't like him and said it was, just to get rid of him. She also told him she didn't want to sell it.'

'A man from the village?'

'She said not, and not Czech either. She was sure of that. I think he may have been Russian. She said he spoke Czech with an accent like yours.'

She thought about it for a moment, before saying, 'Perhaps it is nothing?'

'Perhaps. But we can't ignore it.'

'What do you think we should do, Frank?'

'Be on guard. First, I'm going to check the car over, and consider moving it. Meanwhile, I want you to get ready and be prepared to leave here at very short notice. We may not need to move, but we need to be able to do it if necessary.'

Olga was quiet for a few moments, obviously thinking things over. She had a lot to consider. I left her to it.

* * *

I was in a bit of a quandary. Pull the plug now, or just tough it out? Calling Leon and asking for reinforcements was an option, but not a good one. First, I had no firm grounds for thinking anything had changed here. Bringing in a squad of security staff who might not have anything to do when they arrived, and who would make Olga's presence here even more of a matter of local gossip than it probably already was, wouldn't help. If Olga agreed to that in the first place, of course, which was a pretty big "if".

Second, Leon's resources were likely fully stretched already, given that he had recalled Vladimir and crew despite his concern for Olga. He had brought me in to lift some of the load, not to add to it.

Overall, my thinking was that not enough had really changed. It was all just speculation and suspicion.

Based here, Olga remained highly vulnerable and I believed she would be safer back in Prague. So did Leon. But the lady herself wasn't having that.

So we would carry on as we were. I would do what I could, stay alert, and hope for the best. Perhaps by the time Leon's critical period was over things would be different, but I doubted it.

I turned away and pulled out my phone, which had begun to vibrate in my pocket. What now, I wondered with a grimace. Another crisis?

CHAPTER FORTY-ONE

I saw the caller was Jimmy Mack, and let it go to voicemail. The last thing I wanted was another discussion with Jimmy about Jamie Burke. Not at that moment, anyway. Then I noticed there was another message waiting for me. I decided I'd better listen to them both.

'I'll see you later, Olga. I've got something I need to sort out.'

I waved the phone at her and she nodded.

I went outside, into the fresh air and the cool, wintry sunshine. Then I took a deep breath before listening to my messages.

The first one wasn't from Jimmy Mack. It was from Bill Peart, who had been trying to reach me again.

'Where the hell are you, Frank? I really need to talk to you — urgently! I still haven't seen Burke, and I'm very concerned now. Have you no idea at all where he could be? He might have tucked himself away somewhere, but I'm seriously worried something has happened to him. Call me!'

I grimaced when the message ended. What to do? What to say? I had no more idea than Bill where Jamie was. All I could tell him was what Jimmy Mack had told me: Jamie had called to see me a few days ago. He'd been all right then, but I had no idea how or where he was now.

For a few moments, I pondered calling Bill. Then I decided I'd better hear what Jimmy had to say first.

It wasn't good. But it could have been worse.

'Jamie came again, looking for you. He was in a bit of a state. Said he couldn't go back to his place because they were there, waiting for him. I gather you know who he means.

'Anyway, it ended up with him staying with me overnight, and it looks like he'll be here again tonight. He's told me a bit about the trouble he's in, but he doesn't want me to talk to Bill Peart. What do you think, Frank?'

I closed my eyes and blew out with exasperation. What the hell to do now? I couldn't just leave it in Jimmy's hands, even if it was nothing to do with me. I had to do something to help him out.

When I opened my eyes again, I saw how lovely it was there, how peaceful and quiet, in Olga's garden. The dead grass, pale-coloured and fading away, swayed in a gentle breeze. The kitchen garden, near the house, was done now, but still showed signs of what it had been like a couple of months ago, when the tomatoes and corncobs were closing in on season's end.

I listened to a slow lorry hauling its way up the road from the village, alternately roaring and spluttering as it struggled to cope with load and gradient. A blackbird swooped across the ground in front of me without a warning cry, giving me no more than a token glance. And there was wood smoke in the air from the stoves of nearby cottages. Peace reigned.

All in all, despite it being decidedly chilly, the garden of Olga's house was a good place to be, to rest and to think. After a few minutes of quiet contemplation, an idea emerged that captured my interest.

No, it wasn't possible, I decided with a wry smile. No way. I dismissed the thought with amusement. What nonsense! How could that ever be possible? How stupid of me. Stupid, stupid, stupid!

But the idea couldn't be banished as easily as that. It just wouldn't go away. After another few minutes of struggle, I went back indoors to talk to Olga again.

CHAPTER FORTY-TWO

'Problem?' Olga asked.

I nodded. 'It's not of my making, but it's to do with the friend of a friend of mine. He's in serious trouble, and friends of mine are unable to accept that there are times when I just can't help.'

'Nothing at all you can do? That isn't like you, Frank.'

I gave a rueful smile, and then took a deep breath.

'Actually, I have just thought of a possible way of helping the man in trouble. Doing so would also help us, as well — you and me, that is. I'd like to know what you think.'

What had occurred to me was that I could bring Jamie Burke here. That would get him out of the danger zone, and get him off the backs of Jimmy Mack and Bill Peart.

It would also mean I would have someone to share duties with, a tough character with experience of danger in both battlefield and boxing ring. And a man prepared to stand up for his principles despite being under serious threat.

But it all depended on Olga, and what she thought. She listened to what I had to say and weighed things up for a few moments.

'I agree,' she said. 'That is an excellent plan, Frank. By helping us, your friend's friend will help himself. You must talk to Jamie Burke, and arrange this.'

'I should speak to Leon, as well.'

She shook her head. 'Leon will agree. Like me, he trusts your judgement. But I will let him know what we plan anyway. Jamie can be here with us for a while, and then, when the time comes for him to appear in a law court in England, I am sure Leon will arrange to get him there safely.'

I let out my breath and smiled with relief. Perhaps it hadn't been such a crazy idea after all.

CHAPTER FORTY-THREE

After running things through with Olga some more, I rang Jimmy Mack.

'Is Jamie still with you, Jim?'

'He is. How are you doing, Frank?'

'I'm fine, thanks. Doing Leon's work. I won't say anything about it just now, but I might be able to help Jamie. Can you put him on?'

He broke off to shout for Jamie. I cringed. Jimmy's getting a bit hard of hearing these days, as well as suffering from arthritis. That seems to make him think everyone else is a bit deaf, as well as him, and he needs to bellow. Luckily for him, he has a tolerant next-door neighbour, who is often away from home for extended periods.

'Hi, Frank. How are you doing?'

'All right, Jamie, thanks. Better than you anyway, it seems. What's going on?'

'Oh, it's been difficult. They were watching the house, waiting to move in on me. People sent by Kravertz, I'm sure. I didn't know where to turn. So I upped and left before they saw me. And I haven't been back.

'All I could think of was that you lived not far away, and you'd said to let you know . . . Anyway, I'm sorry. I just

148

couldn't think of anything else. So I came looking for you. But Jimmy said you were away, working?'

'That's right. I am. You've been staying with Jimmy, I gather?'

'Yeah. He's a good man. He offered to let me stay overnight. Now I've stayed another night, as well.'

'It can't go on, Jamie. It's too much to put on him. He's an old feller. What are you thinking of doing?'

'No idea, really. Not yet anyway.'

'I take it you're ruling out asking the police for help, or going back with Witness Protection?'

'Yeah. I'm not doing that again. I don't trust any of them. They're a bunch of . . .'

'All right, all right!' I snapped, as his voice rose. 'I get the message.'

'It's how it is,' he said with resignation.

'Henry wanted me to help you, Jamie, but I can't do anything about the situation there. I might be able to help you in another way, though.'

'Oh? How?'

Now was the time for me to think again, and to decide if this really was a good idea. I did think again, for a moment, but my mind didn't change.

'You've done some security work, you told me?'

'Security work? Well, yes. That's what I did for KOSC.'

'What kind?'

'All sorts, onshore and offshore. Protecting property. Protecting people. Guarding things. Run-of-the-mill, if you like. Why do you ask?'

'There's an opportunity for you to join me here, if you're interested. My current job is providing personal security for someone who is at risk for the next three weeks or so. I know the person concerned, and I'm happy with the job. But it's too much for one man. I could do with a helping hand.

'I can't do 24/7 on my own, obviously, and that's what's really needed. So I want someone to share the load. If you're interested, I think you would be a good fit, from what I know and what I've heard.

'So far as the job's concerned — I can't hide it — there's risk involved, serious risk. On the other hand, conditions are good and you would be well paid. Possibly more important than any of that, though, from your point of view, is that you would be out of the country. You'd be well away from Kravertz and KOSC.

'Anyway, that's the situation, and the offer. It's up to you to consider if you want to take it.'

'Where is it? Where are you?'

'I'm not going to tell you that unless you say you want the job. All I'll say for now is that it's abroad, and somewhere in Europe.

'Anyway, that's the best I can do for you, Jamie. Think about it, and weigh my offer against any other options you have, or that you can come up with. I'm not going to give you long to think about it, though. It's nine in the morning now, where you are. I'll ring back at noon. You can give me your answer then, one way or the other.'

'OK, Frank,' he said hesitantly. 'And thanks for thinking of me.'

'Oh, I'm thinking of me as much as you, Jamie! Don't you worry about that.'

CHAPTER FORTY-FOUR

'Did you call him?' Olga asked when I went back inside.

'Yes. I've given him until noon today to think about it. I'll call him again then.'

'Perhaps he will have a better offer?' she said with a smile. 'As you have found, working for the Podolsky family is not much fun at times.'

'It's also dangerous at times,' I pointed out with a chuckle. 'No, I'm sure that won't come into it.'

'What have you told him about the work?'

'I've told him very little. Just that it's about personal protection. He's done that sort of thing before. So he'll know what to expect. I haven't said where the job is, though, or where I am right now. Just that it's somewhere in Europe. So if he declines the offer, I've not exposed anything about you or the situation here.'

She mulled it over for a moment, and then said, 'Do you think he will want to come?'

'Hard to say.' I shrugged. 'He would be a fool not to, in my opinion. He's on his own, and he'll likely spend the next few months, or even much longer, constantly looking over his shoulder if he stays in England.

'Besides, the best time of his life seems to have been when he was in the army. He enjoyed that. Things weren't so good for him before then, and haven't been much better since, from what he says. If he does join us, I think he might like it here.'

'You are very supportive of him, Frank?'

'Well, he's a lifelong friend of a good friend of mine. They both started life in an orphanage, without parents, and things haven't been easy for either of them.

'The trouble Jamie found himself in was not of his own making, and the danger he's in now is because he's determined to do the right thing, and help bring an evil man down.'

'Who is that?'

'His boss at the offshore company where he was working, a company called KOSC, which is owned by a Daniel Kravertz. Although I don't know Jamie well, I have to say that I did like him when we met. I think he's a good man.'

'I understand,' Olga said. 'I hope I get to meet Jamie Burke. Now, Frank, you must go for a walk, and let me get on with my work. I have much to do. Think about how to get Jamie here, if he decides to come, and how the Podolsky family can help.'

I smiled and left her to it. No one can dismiss a man as gently as Olga Podolsky can.

* * *

At twelve sharp, I called Jimmy Mack's number again.

'Is he still there, Jim?'

'Aye. He's here. Are you going to help him?'

'It's up to him now. Can you put him on?'

The phone changed hands.

'Frank?'

'Hi, Jamie. Have you decided what you want to do?'

'Is the offer still open?'

'It is.'

'Then I'd like to join you.'
'Good! Right, let's get down to business.'

* * *

For the next few minutes, we talked about what he needed to do, and how to do it.

'First, have you got a passport?'

'Well . . . I have one. But it's in the house.'

'You'll need it. Can you get it?'

As he hesitated, I said, 'Go there in broad daylight, Jamie. There'll likely be plenty of people about. Anyone watching the house won't dare touch you then. You can be in and out in a minute or two.

'Don't bother with collecting anything else. Just get the passport. That's all you need. Everything else you can pick up at the airport, or get it here.'

'OK,' he said, sounding a bit dubious.

I could understand that. He was jumping off a cliff edge into the unknown. Still, as a former soldier, he might well have jumped out of planes in his time. This wasn't going to be that bad.

'Where's your car?'

'Skinningrove. I left it down there when I realised they were watching the house.'

I thought quickly, working out what he could do.

'That's fine, Jamie. Very good, in fact. Look, I know your terrace. Come in the back way, from Downdinner Hill, and across the fields to the path at the back of the houses. They probably won't be watching that side. When you leave, go up the road to Hummersea and then along the clifftop path to Skinningrove. You'll soon see if anyone is following you. If they're not, just pick up your car in Skinningrove, drive straight to Newcastle airport and leave it in long-term parking. I'll get back to you as soon as I can about your travel arrangements from there. If necessary, you can stay overnight in a hotel at the airport.'

'Yes,' he said, sounding more confident now. 'That should work. Where am I going, by the way?'

'Prague.'

'Czechoslovakia?'

'Well, where you're coming to used to be part of it. Now this part is called the Czech Republic.'

'Oh, yes. I'd forgotten about that.'

'You won't be staying in Prague,' I added. 'You'll be collected in arrivals by someone holding a card bearing the name . . . "Mr Morgan", let's say. Not your own name, remember!

'And that's all you really need to know right now. Hopefully, we'll get you a flight for tomorrow, either morning or evening. I'll let you know the details when I have them. Any questions?'

'No. You've covered things pretty well, thanks.'

'Good. Welcome aboard, Jamie!'

CHAPTER FORTY-FIVE

Using my phone, I managed to book and pay for a seat for Jamie on a flight for Prague leaving Newcastle the next morning. Then I rang him at Jimmy Mack's again and gave him the details.

'You can collect the tickets at the airport, and check in whenever you like from now on. Have you got a phone, by the way?'

'In my pocket.'

'Give me your number, to stop Jimmy complaining about us wearing his phone out and giving him a big bill.'

Jamie chuckled. 'I don't believe he would. Jimmy's a very kind and easy-going guy.'

'Until you get on the wrong side of him! I can tell you now, you don't ever want to do that.'

'I'll remember,' he said solemnly.

'Right, then. I'll see you tomorrow, Jamie. But let me know when you've got your passport and are on your way. Just text me.'

'Will do.'

I didn't tell him to call me if anything went wrong. That would have been too much like tempting fate.

* * *

Next stop was to arrange for someone from the Podolsky organisation to collect Jamie from Vaclav Havel Airport. I left that to Olga to sort out. She assured me there wouldn't be a problem, and got right on with it.

* * *

Leon called me later, having already spoken to Olga.

'The new man you want to bring in, Frank. That's fine. I understand why you're doing it. You need some help, and bringing him in will help you and Olga as well as the man himself. Like Olga, I trust your judgement about him.'

'Thanks, Leon. It should work out fine. I know you would probably have made someone available if I had asked for help, but this is a better solution. It will help me and him.

'Also, if there were to be an emergency, I would rather have a man with me who speaks my language like a native, someone from my own part of the country as well.'

Leon chuckled. 'I understand, Frank. He'll be collected at the airport and brought over to you. There shouldn't be a problem.'

'How is Charles, by the way? Is he still in danger?'

'He's not good, but the doctors believe he is out of danger now.'

'That's good news!'

'Yes, it is. Recovery will be slow, of course, and perhaps only partial. We'll just have to be patient, and wait and see.

'Frank, there's just something I wanted to ask you about the new man. You've said he has military and security industry experience, which sounds good. You also told Olga that he worked for an offshore company that dismantles oil rigs?'

'Yes, that's right. And that's where he ran into trouble.'

'Do you know the name of the company?'

'Yes. Kravertz Offshore Construction — or KOSC.'

'Oh? Is that right?'

'You sound surprised, Leon. Have you heard of them?'

'Based on Teesside, aren't they?'

'Yes,' I said, surprised myself now.

'I know a little about them, from the Admiralty, and it's not good. So Jamie Burke is tied up with the attempts to investigate and prosecute the KOSC owner, eh?'

'That's right.'

All this made me wonder what Leon was doing right now, and where he was.

'Are you still at sea, Leon?'

'For the moment. Still aboard the trawler you didn't like. There is much work for us to do. That is all I will say for now. But I must talk to Jamie when he arrives. He may know things that would help me.'

'OK, Leon. No problem.'

We ended the conversation with me wondering what was going on. What could Jamie Burke possibly know that might help Leon Podolsky?

CHAPTER FORTY-SIX

Kámen

Jamie was in good spirits when he arrived. He got out of the car that had brought him and turned to me with a big grin on his face.

'Hi, Frank! How are you doing?'

'I'm doing fine,' I said reaching out to shake his hand. 'How about you? Journey OK?'

'Wonderful! I enjoyed every bit of it. I did what you'd suggested at the Loftus end, by the way. That worked well. Then I got myself to Newcastle airport without a problem, and everything went smoothly in Prague, as well.'

I couldn't help thinking that sounded a lot better experience than I'd had on arrival.

'This is Mirek, by the way,' Jamie said, as the driver appeared alongside us. 'He was waiting for me at the airport.'

'Good morning!' Mirek said with a smile, as he reached out to shake my hand. 'It is me again.'

'Hello!' I said with surprise, adding for Jamie's benefit that we had already met.

This was the man who had mysteriously appeared alongside to help when I was tending to Charles outside the airport.

'Thank you for bringing Jamie here,' I told him.

'It was a pleasure,' he said, still smiling. 'I enjoyed the opportunity to use the English language, which I know only from the classes I attend.'

'It must be a pretty good language school, in that case,' I told him. 'Do they teach Englishmen Czech, too? I ought to sign up with them if they do.'

'He speaks better English than me,' Jamie added, making Mirek laugh.

They had obviously got on well together on their trip. Leon had chosen the right man for the job.

'Now I must return to Prague,' Mirek announced.

'Will you have coffee with us, or stay for a meal?' I asked.

He shook his head. 'There is much to do in Prague. You know how it is with Leon, I believe?'

'Oh, yes,' I assured him with a chuckle. 'I do know. He's a busy man.'

'All the time,' Mirek agreed. 'Busy all the time.'

With that, he left.

* * *

Jamie glanced around and said, 'This is where we're based, is it, Frank?'

'It is.'

'Looks an interesting old place.'

'Yes, it is. Good to see you, by the way. You're looking well.'

He shrugged. 'I can't tell you how glad I am to be here, Frank. Things had got me down a bit, back there. So thanks again for offering me an escape route.'

'Well, I couldn't do much for you back in England. And I needed a good man to help me here. It was a happy coincidence. I thought we could help each other.

'Let me tell you what we're doing. We're safeguarding a woman called Olga Podolsky, who runs the IT side of a big family business. Her brother, Leon, is the head of it.

'The family were spread across Russia and Ukraine. Other places, as well, in the days of the Soviet Union. But they emigrated to this country when that became possible and became Czech citizens. I've known them — or some of them, and their descendants — for a few years, and I've worked for them a number of times. They always have security issues.

'Leon asked me to come and look after Olga for a short while. She's always at risk because of the work she does, and her importance to the family business, but right now the risk is at a high level. It's a short-term job, protecting her ahead of a crisis deadline on December sixteenth. Not even a few weeks away now.'

'Who is she at risk from?'

'A good question, Jamie. I don't really know the answer to that, and I'm not sure they do either. At times, it's been organised crime gangs, and at other times, agents of the Russian state. Right now, we're on high alert because of work the Podolskys are doing for the UK government in the North Sea.'

'Oh?'

He seemed as surprised by that as I had been.

'You're thinking we're a long way from there?'

'Well, yes. A very long way.'

'Put it down to the wonders of modern technology.'

Studying him, I added, 'Are you OK with all this, Jamie? If you're not, you're free to go. I wouldn't want you to stay otherwise.'

He shrugged. 'No need to worry about that, Frank. I'm glad to have the chance to be here. I just hope I can do some good.'

'I'm sure you can. Right, now that's out of the way, let's go inside and I'll introduce you to Olga.'

CHAPTER FORTY-SEVEN

'Welcome, Jamie!' Olga said with a big smile. 'I am so glad you have been able to come here to join us, and to help Frank. Protecting me is far too much for one man.'

Jamie chuckled and shook her outstretched hand. 'I'm very happy to be here,' he assured her.

'I'll leave it to Frank to show you around the house, and to tell you what he is doing. For now, let me just say that you are to make yourself at home here, as much as that is possible.'

'Thank you.'

* * *

I led Jamie away from the basement, where Olga was ensconced as usual, and was obviously busy.

'She seems a nice woman,' he confided.

'Oh, she is!' I chuckled and added, 'That makes protecting her an honour rather than a duty. Come on! Let me show you around. By the way, you don't have any luggage to drop off, do you?'

He shook his head. 'I only have what I'm wearing. I took your advice.'

'That's fine. We'll do some shopping for you later.'

'You don't need to buy me anything, Frank. I've got money, and I don't need much anyway. But I would like to get a few things.'

'A toothbrush?'

'That, as well.'

'We'll get it sorted. Now, the house — and your room.'

* * *

I was pleased so far with Jamie. He seemed relaxed, and he was handling himself well on what had been a bit of a roll-ercoaster ride for him. I put that down to his relief at having been pulled out of the danger area. Here, he was a new man — his own man again. For now, at least, he was free from constant fear.

As I showed him around the house and garden, I out-lined the potential problems and told him what I'd been trying to do.

'What you've been doing makes sense,' he said, nod-ding. 'Is Olga under a serious threat?'

'She is — believe me! The Podolskys have some serious enemies and rivals.'

'It's hard to believe Olga could have them, though, from what I've seen of her.'

'It's not personal. Her enemies are not interested in her as a human being. All they care about is her role in the Podolsky business empire. Hit Olga, and it would be hard for it to keep going.'

'What kind of business is it?'

'The core is financial, but they have all sorts of other interests, some related, others not. They own a hotel and a medical centre in Prague, for example. Also, they oper-ate a subscription advisory service for people moving money around the world. And now, it seems, they own ships, ocean-going research vessels.'

'What are they doing with them?'

I shrugged. 'All I know is that Leon is currently aboard one and has a contract with the British Admiralty to do some work in the North Sea.'

'Impressive.'

I nodded agreement. 'By the way, Leon was interested to learn that you worked for KOSC. He wants to find time to talk to you about that.'

'No worries. I'll happily tell him everything I know.'

'Yeah. I thought you might say something like that,' I said, chuckling.

CHAPTER FORTY-EIGHT

With Jamie here, I could share out the duties, especially watch-keeping at night, and do a bit more planning.

'So far,' I told him, 'it's been difficult at night. The sensors around the perimeter are a form of insurance, but they're not infallible. Someone needs to be on watch.'

'Not easy to do for one man,' he said with a chuckle, 'not if you have to stay awake all day as well.'

'You're darned right!'

'Well, I'm used to night shifts, Frank. I don't mind being nightwatchman.'

I shook my head. 'No. That wouldn't be right. We'll take turns. Swap over every other night or two. We'll both get some decent sleep that way.'

'Suits me,' he said with a shrug. 'I'll be doing a lot better than for a long time.'

'Now, though, Jamie, I want you to get outside and wander around on your own a bit. Familiarise yourself with the property, and the immediate surrounds. See if there's any way we could be doing things better.

'You'll see what we've done to improve the fencing. That and the sensors are about all we have done, though. There was some exploratory drilling for an emergency tunnel from the house, but the construction crew had to pull out for a couple of weeks before work really got started.

'What I'm going to do next is get Olga to help me plan an emergency escape route out of the house. We're only here for a few weeks, if things go to plan, but she'll be here by herself long after that if things go well.'

'On her own?' Jamie asked, looking and sounding surprised.

I nodded. 'That's how she likes it. Her brother would prefer to have her holed up under guard in Prague, but she won't hear of it. She wants to live here in the country, independently. And I was the only security presence she would accept. For some misguided reason known only to her, she seems to think a lot of me and my capabilities.'

'It seems really strange that she wants to be here on her own, when there's so much risk for her,' Jamie said, shaking his head.

'It is. I agree totally. But when you get to know Olga, you'll understand it a bit better. She tries to live as normal a life as possible, and she likes to live in a humble way among ordinary people. The billionaire lifestyle that her brother has is not for her. She's happy with her own company, and she accepts the risk that goes with living alone. The rest of the family, who love her dearly, have also had to accept it.'

'Is she . . . ?'

He faltered, not quite able to get the word out. I wondered if the word he had in mind was *mad*.

'No, she isn't,' I said with a smile. 'Not at all. She's just a bit special.'

CHAPTER FORTY-NINE

Olga was taking a breather when I went to see her, as it happened, and was quite ready to do a circuit of the house with me as I tried to figure out an emergency exit plan.

'How's it going?' I asked her. 'Found anything?'

'No. Nothing much out of the ordinary so far. It's very worrying. We're running out of time. Less than three weeks to go. I'm starting to wonder if we're missing something, something obvious.'

I grimaced, but there was nothing I could do to help. I had to focus on the situation here, right now.

'I don't want to give you even more worries, Olga, but I'd like you to help me work out an emergency escape route out of the house.'

'Oh?'

'It's always best to have one, just in case. I even have one from my cottage.'

'Really? But you live in such a peaceful place.'

'That has never stopped unpeaceful people turning up from time to time. But it's not just people you have to worry about. You also have to think of natural dangers, like fire.' I shrugged and added, 'It's just worst-case scenario planning.'

'So what is your escape strategy — from your cottage on the beautiful Cleveland coast in England?'

'Well, I didn't invent it. I found it. A long time ago, other people living there must have felt they needed an emergency escape route. So they built a tunnel from the cottage to the nearby cliff face. From there, you can get down to the little beach below. The access to the tunnel is via a trapdoor in the floor of the porch at the back of my cottage.'

'How interesting! I wonder what the original owners were afraid of?'

'I don't know for sure, but I think they might have been smugglers. In that case, it would have been the Government's Customs and Excise officials they were worried about. A lot of other people along the Cleveland coast also had to be on guard at the time. Smuggling was a hanging offence back then.'

'Oh, my goodness! Is their example why you thought of building a tunnel here?'

'Probably. But until Vladimir comes back to build us one, we need another way to exit the house.'

'How very logical!' she said with a smile. 'Come on, then. Let us see what we can find.'

* * *

'What's up there?' I asked, pointing at a small trapdoor in the ceiling of the corridor where our bedrooms were.

'Who knows?' Olga said, shrugging.

'It must be a loft, or attic.'

'Yes, I think so.'

'I wonder what's in it?'

'I have not looked,' she said with another shrug.

'I'll find a ladder and go up later.'

'There is a stepladder in the basement. You could use that.'

'OK. That's good.'

We moved on.

* * *

The basement was the strongest part of the house. The walls were made of ancient stone blocks, now reinforced with concrete, and were a good two feet thick. They were the foundations of the entire structure above ground. From the entrance hall of the house, a flight of stone steps led down to a very strong-looking steel door that gave entrance to the basement, most of which was now the computer room.

'This obviously wasn't the original door,' I said, smoothing my hand over the immaculate surface.

'Oh, no!' Olga laughed at the thought. 'That was made of wood, and had largely rotted away. We installed this new door. It is the only entrance to the computer room, and to the rest of the basement. We wanted it to be strong, which is why we chose one made of steel.'

'How does it work?' I asked, seeing no furniture on the surface of the door.

'The door knows me,' she said with a smile. 'It opens when I come, and closes when I leave. Watch!'

She stepped closer, and I watched the door slide silently aside. It then closed again when she stepped back.

'Impressive,' I said. 'Modern technology, eh?'

* * *

When, or if, a tunnel ever got built, there would need to be access to it from the basement. That would require some heavy-duty work, to break through the stone wall, but it could be done. Right now, though, there wasn't a tunnel. So all that was for the future. We needed to improvise an emergency exit for the here and now.

When we had finished the tour of the house, I went with Olga to collect the stepladder from the basement, intending to have a look in the loft.

'Prepare to be amazed when you get up there,' she said with a smile. 'Such places in these old houses can be places time has forgotten.'

'Then if I'm not back in half an hour, you'd better send out a search party.'

Olga had spoken in jest, but she was dead right. I was amazed. The loft was so big and high that it was like entering the nave of a church, or it would have been if it had been empty. It was a vast space beneath a steeply sloping roof. At one time, it would have seemed cavernous; it would have echoed with my presence. Not now, though. Now it was more like a warehouse, absolutely brimming with the stuff stored, or just abandoned, there.

For a start, there must have been a ton of cement, in paper sacks stacked as high as me on pallets. Then there were bicycles that would have been more usefully kept in a shed in the garden. Stacks of used car tyres, too. And piles of miscellaneous tools — anvils, jacks, saws, sledgehammers . . . You name it! They were all there.

I also saw pallets laden with foodstuffs in commercial-size tins, bags and sacks — flour and rice, sugar and coffee, lentils and potatoes. And stacks of big plastic water bottles, too. I shook my head in awe. This was survivors' paradise. A considerable number of people could have lived and dined here for months on end.

I moved through it all, checking the walls and roof, looking for a safe way out that didn't involve returning through the trapdoor in the ceiling of the corridor. It wasn't easy, but I managed to work one out eventually. Satisfied for now, I returned to what passed for the normal world down below.

CHAPTER FIFTY

Now that Jamie was here, and had slotted into the groove nicely, I decided it was time I called Bill Peart again and put him out of his misery. I knew it would be no fun to be responsible for someone's safety, but be unable to find the guy.

'Where are you now?' he said gruffly, when he answered the phone.

'And a very good morning to you too, Bill!'

'What do you want?'

I grinned. He was in fine fettle.

'I want to put you out of your misery with regard to Jamie Burke.'

'You've seen him?'

'I have. He's fine. You don't need to worry about him for the time being.'

'Oh?'

He could tell something was coming, some hammer blow that would shatter his morning peace. At least, that was what he clearly feared.

'I've called you on your personal mobile, Bill, for a good reason. If you're not in a position to receive information that

170

I need you to keep quiet, I'll stop now. All I'll tell you is that Jamie is safe and well, which is the important part anyway.'

'Call me back in twenty minutes,' he said.

* * *

Next, I went looking for Jamie, who was out scanning our perimeter defences.

'Found anything?'

He shook his head. 'Nothing at all. Everything is in good shape. No sign of anybody suspicious hanging around, or anything like that, either.'

'What I like to hear!'

'Not a bad morning, is it?' he added.

I agreed, and looked round at the cold, still day with mist down in the valley and the sun promising to break through over the hilltops above the forest.

'It's going to get out,' I added, 'according to the forecast.'

Jamie grinned. 'Are the forecasters here any better than that lot we have?'

'Actually, you'll no doubt be surprised to hear, the Czech forecasts are pretty good. This is a continental country a long way from the Atlantic, which gives the UK so much turbulence. So the weather here is more predictable than ours. It's generally the same and pretty stable, right across the country. You don't get the regional variations we're used to.'

'Hmm,' he said, sounding unconvinced, but not wanting to say so.

I smiled. His attitude was fine. It was what I wanted to see. Gentle agnosticism. Making his own mind up. Independence of thought. That was what I needed from him. I didn't want an ex-squaddy, yes-sir, no-sir routine. I needed Jamie to be an extra pair of eyes and ears, and an alert, independent brain.

Although he hadn't seemed like that when I first met him back at home, I'd hoped he would be that way out here. The signs were already looking good.

'Jamie, there's something I want to talk to you about. I have a pal in Cleveland Police, DI Bill Peart. He's been worried lately, because he's supposed to be keeping an eye on you, but he hasn't seen you for a while.'

'He called at the house one time.'

'I believe he did. Anyway, he's called me a couple of times, asking if I knew where you were. I didn't tell him anything at first. In fact, I didn't know where you were until you fetched up at Jimmy Mack's.

'But now you're here, and getting settled, I want to let him know you're with me. So he can stop worrying.'

That got Jamie worried.

'Tell the police? They leak!'

I shook my head. 'That won't happen in this case. I trust Bill to keep secret what I tell him in private. He's a good pal. Anyway, it can't leak. All Bill knows is that I'm abroad somewhere. He doesn't know where, and I won't tell him. It's better for us both like that. There are times when I don't want him to know something, and times when he doesn't need or want to know. So don't fear your whereabouts will be leaked. I just wanted you to know what I'm doing. I don't want you to start thinking I'm doing things behind your back.'

'OK, Frank. I wouldn't think that anyway, not after what you've done for me.'

With that, I left him to it and went off to make another call to Bill.

* * *

'So he's with you, is he?'

'He is now, yes. He was desperate and turned up at Risky Point. Jimmy Mack phoned to let me know.'

'Humph. He didn't let me know.'

'Well, he would have known Jamie didn't want the police involved, in case there's another leak. I'm not going to tell you where he is now, either. All I wanted was to let you know there's no need for you to worry. He's OK. And he's well.'

172

'How about you? Are you happy with all this?'

'Yes. I couldn't help him back there, but I needed an extra pair of hands here and I thought he might fit the bill. So we're both happy.'

'What about the court proceedings?'

'I'll talk to you nearer the time about that. One way or another, though, we'll get him there safely. I can promise you that. OK?'

'Well . . . For now, it is, I suppose. I'll just let the chief know he's abroad somewhere, somewhere safe. And I'm assured he'll be back for the trial. That will have to do.'

'Cheer up, Bill! That will have to do. There's nothing else for it.'

'We could arrest him, and hold him as an essential witness.'

'Only if you could arrange extradition. How long would extradition proceedings take, do you think? A year? Two years? You might as well just wait for him to return in his own time.'

'Point made,' Bill said, with a heavy sigh. 'We're festooned with lawyers in this country. By the way, if you're not here, when are we going to have that day out fishing we talked about? That's what I'd really like to know.'

'Soon, I hope, Bill,' I told him with a wry smile. 'Soon would be good.'

CHAPTER FIFTY-ONE

Bynovec, a village near Kámen
9 December

'What are you saying?' Kravertz demanded.

Patiently, Jed Smith said, 'Like I told you, boss, he's here. Burke.'

'That's not funny, Jed. Don't make jokes like that. We're in trouble here — both of us, not just me! I'm not in the mood for jokes. If we can't sort this business out for Manny, everything we've been working for goes down the tubes. The company, me, you — every damn thing!'

'I've seen him!' Smith protested. 'No joke. He's here.'

Kravertz stared hard, and somehow managed to hold back his mounting rage. It took him a minute or two. Smith's own stare never wavered.

'For real? You've seen him?'

Smith nodded.

'Where?'

'In the garden of that house we're watching, where the Russian woman lives. I haven't seen the woman, but I've seen Burke. It looks like he's living there.'

Kravertz sat down to think about it. He was coming round to believe Jed. At least, to believe he wasn't joking. He might be mistaken, and probably was, but he seemed to really believe he'd seen Burke.

He had to think about this. If Jed was right, it was a game changer. It was more than he could have hoped for. Burke here? As well as the Russian woman? God knew how it had happened, but he wasn't going to miss out on the best opportunity he'd had in a long while.

He'd had to go along with Manny about the priorities, but maybe something good had come of that anyway. Both of them here!

'What do you want to do, boss?'

Kravertz looked up, smiled and said, 'Go get him, Jed! Take some of the Czechs and grab Burke.'

CHAPTER FIFTY-TWO

Olga's house

With the two of us now to share duties and keep an eye on things, it was possible to relax and have a little free time. It was good to be able to wander around the village without pressure to get back to the house fast. And sleep at night became possible, too, as we took turns to keep watch. What a relief it all was.

Everything was new to Jamie, of course. He enjoyed looking around, seeing how things worked and how people here lived. I was happy to let him do it. Pulling him out of Loftus, and out of the strain he'd been under for so long, was working wonders. He was a new man. Even Olga noticed.

'Jamie seems to like it here,' she observed.

'You've seen that, as well, have you?'

She nodded. 'It's easy to tell when someone is content and enjoying life. Also, of course, he works very hard. I think you made a good choice, Frank. I'm glad you brought him here.'

'I think so, too. He's helping us, and we're helping him.'

'Perfect,' she concluded with a smile.

'I'm just going to visit the little shop, Olga. It will be closing soon, and there's something I need. I'll only be a few minutes, and Jamie will be back soon anyway.'

'Yes, you go, Frank. Be sure to wear your good coat. It is not so warm now.'

I shook my head, but smiled as well. Olga was behaving like Mother Hen, now she had the two of us to look after.

* * *

I had only gone a few yards from the gate when I spotted Jamie in the distance, toiling up the hill towards me. He'd done another circuit of the village, I assumed, and now was heading back to base to report and re-water. I was about to give him a wave when a big van that had just passed me pulled up alongside him. He paused and turned towards it, no doubt ready to tell the driver that he didn't speak the language, and in any case was a stranger here, and probably couldn't help.

He didn't get to do that. A door in the side of the van slid open and several men piled out and immediately began attacking him. It looked like they were trying to force him inside the van. He wasn't having that, and fought back fiercely.

I saw one man slump to the ground, felled by what looked like a classic straight left to the head. A roundhouse swing was landed on another guy. As the others redoubled their efforts, I grabbed a lump of old fence post and broke into a run.

Jamie stood his ground well. He was managing to stay on his feet against three big men hammering away at him, but without help he wasn't going to last long.

Roaring like a madman, I got there and slammed into the back of one man with the point of the fence post, using it like a lance and sending him sprawling. Swinging round with the post, I cracked another in the head. Then somebody hit me hard from behind, making me drop the thing and sending me staggering.

Jamie had gone down by then. I managed to get to him and stood over him, hitting out wildly at whoever appeared in front of me until Jamie struggled back to his feet.

Then the driver of the van blew a long blast on the horn. That was a signal that thankfully brought it all to an end. The gang broke away, dragging their wounded with them, and climbed back aboard. Jamie and I held each other upright, both of us heaving for breath and spitting out muck and blood. The van departed with a roar, spraying us with a shower of gravel.

'You OK?' I gasped eventually, straightening up and gently shaking Jamie.

He just grunted in reply.

'Hurt?'

He shook his head. Then he looked up and gave me a crooked grin. 'Bastards!' he snarled.

I nodded with relief. He was all right.

And so was I. Both of us were a bit battered, but we'd survived and given a good account of ourselves.

'Thanks, Frank.'

I just nodded.

We were both still breathing heavily, but speech was becoming possible again.

'Good you turned up,' Jamie added with a gasp.

'Pure luck,' I assured him. 'You were doing OK. But it wasn't a fair fight.'

'You're right there. How many of 'em were there?'

'Oh . . . about twenty, I think.'

'Only twenty? There was more than that!'

I had to grin. 'Yeah. Maybe a few more, now I think about it. Come on! Let's get back to the house.'

'Bastards!' he muttered again as we set off. 'Who the hell were they?'

I just shook my head. No point guessing.

Of one thing I was sure, though. The attack hadn't been an accident. It wasn't just an opportunistic bit of random thuggery or attempted theft. The gang had gone for Jamie deliberately. To my mind, that had to be connected to the reason we were here. And that probably meant they had located Olga.

'You're bleeding,' I said as we trailed back up the hill.

'Not as much as I sometimes was in . . .'

'The ring? I know, I know! Let's you and me exchange war stories.'

'Anyway,' he added, 'so are you.'

'So am I what?'

'Bleeding.'

I wiped an exploratory hand across my face.

'Damn. I thought something was getting in my eyes. We'd both better get cleaned up before Olga sees us.'

'Or she'll think we're not much good as bodyguards.'

'Well, we were outnumbered, remember, Jamie. Don't forget to tell her that.'

As we went through the gate, Jamie paused a moment and then said, 'I know one of them.'

'One of the gang?'

He nodded.

CHAPTER FIFTY-THREE

'Come on, then! Don't keep me in suspense,' I said, wondering if I'd misheard or misunderstood.

'I'm pretty sure it was Jed Smith. In fact, I'm certain it was.'

'Who's he?'

'One of Kravertz's security guys. The main one, in fact. He's always with him. Kravertz and him shot the divers.'

I had stopped by then, astonished. I turned to look at him. 'Are you sure?'

'Yes, I am.' He nodded, and added, 'He was the big guy with the ginger beard. You can't mistake him.'

There had been a bloke that description would fit. I could picture him. He was the one I hit first with the fence post. But how was it possible for it to be the same man Jamie knew back on Teesside?

'If you're right,' I said heavily, 'I don't know what the hell to make of it.'

'Me neither,' Jamie admitted.

'What could he possibly be doing here?'

Again, nothing but a head shake from Jamie.

'Did you see anyone else you knew, or was it just him?'

'Just Smith.'

We stood there in silence for a few moments while I tried to make sense of it. How could Jamie be right? What could a man from an offshore company based on Teesside be doing here? It was so wildly improbable that it seemed a ridiculous idea. But Jamie wasn't backtracking. He was sticking to what he'd said. I couldn't ignore it.

I wondered if Jamie could have led him here, despite the precautions we had taken. Surely they couldn't have tracked him to Newcastle airport, then to Prague and after that to here? Surely not? Next to impossible. To Prague, maybe, unlikely as it seemed, but not all the way to Kámen.

Yet it was Jamie the gang had tried to abduct, and it had been a targeted attack. It was definitely him they had been after.

Could I have misjudged him? Had he informed somebody where he was going, or where he was when he got here? Accidentally, perhaps? Obviously, it was possible, and had to be considered.

'Jamie, have you told anyone back in England where you were going, or where you are?'

'No one.'

He pulled out his phone and held it out to me.

'You can check, if you like. But it's dead anyway now. It needs charging, and I didn't bring the charger with me.'

I shook my head, rejecting the offer.

Where that left me was wondering if the gang could be here for Olga, not Jamie. Ignoring Smith's presence for the moment, that seemed likely. Then they could just have spotted Jamie around the house and targeted him because they wanted information about the set-up here.

But Smith's presence couldn't really be ignored. Logic said that the only way a man who worked for a Teesside offshore company could be here, assisting the search for Olga, was if the company he worked for was associated with the people in this country looking for her.

But how likely was that? Not very.

On the other hand, how likely was it that the Podolskys could be working for the British Admiralty on a project in the North Sea? And if one was possible, and actual, why not the other as well?

'Come on, Jamie! I need to talk to Olga.'

* * *

We got cleaned up first, and then I gave Olga a brief outline of what had happened.

'How is Jamie?' she asked with a grimace.

'All right, I think. He says he had a lot worse when he was boxing.'

'Hmm. You were right about him being a tough man. He did well to stand up to them. Does he want to leave us now?'

'No way! He wants to do the job he signed up for.'

She gave a wan smile at that.

'And you, Frank? I see you've got a nasty wound on your head.'

'That's nothing. It's stopped bleeding.'

'I can look at it . . .'

'No, thanks. It's not necessary.' I drew breath and continued, 'I was just surprised by the attack. Broad daylight. Out in the open. I couldn't see why they went for Jamie, anyway.'

'Perhaps they just wanted information from him, because they knew he was from this house?'

'Perhaps. But it's worse than that, actually. What I haven't told you is that Jamie recognised one of the men. He says the man is from England, and he works for Kravertz, the owner of the company Jamie used to work for.'

'That would be KOSC?'

I nodded. Then I watched as she put the pieces together. She did it faster than I had.

'So Mr Kravertz has found allies in this country?'

'That's what it looks like.'

'Perhaps my peaceful time here is at an end,' she said with a sigh of resignation. 'It had to happen, unfortunately. It always does.'

'I think you're right,' I admitted. 'How I see it is that they didn't come here for Jamie. They couldn't have tracked him all the way to Kámen, even if they had somehow found out he was in this country.'

She nodded and, looking thoughtful, said, 'They came for me, didn't they? Somehow they discovered that I am here.'

I said I had to agree.

'What it means,' I added, 'is that the owner of KOSC must have a relationship with people in this country who want to bring the Podolskys down.'

'Yes. Leon believes there is such a link.'

'Oh? With international organised crime?'

She shrugged. 'Who knows? There may well be a state behind it all.'

Russia, in other words. I had to hope not.

I didn't say any of the obvious things I could have said then. Olga had heard them all before, I was sure. Probably many times. This was no way to live. If she wasn't such a stubborn, determined individual, she would have taken the advice long ago. My heart went out to her.

'But I will not leave here,' she said, as if reading my thoughts. 'Not yet anyway. I must complete the work I am doing. Then I will think about things again.'

You couldn't deny her courage. And my determination to protect her was, if anything, strengthened. We would see it through. If Olga could stay, so could Jamie and I.

CHAPTER FIFTY-FOUR

Bynovec

The attempted abduction didn't work. But it did settle Kravertz's mind. Pictures on a mobile phone confirmed what Jed Smith had told him. He wasn't deluded or mistaken. Burke was here, right now. And so was the Podolsky woman.

Kravertz shook his head, scarcely able to believe it. No catch! They were both here, together, in the same place. It was as if Christmas and his birthday had come together in one joyous celebration. Both his and Manny's priorities could be dealt with at one and the same time.

As for why and how the two targets were both here, he had no idea. He didn't care, either. But he did know what he wanted done about it.

'No more surveillance,' he said to Smith, and to Zeman. 'No more pissing about, watching and waiting. We're going to hit that house and take out both of them.'

'When?' Smith asked.

'Tonight. Let's get it done.'

'Right.'

'That will be good,' Zeman said with obvious approval. 'Then we can get back to our own business.'

'And we can get back to ours,' Kravertz assured him. 'There's just one thing you should know,' he added. 'I know what you said earlier, but I don't want the woman captured. I want her eliminated.'

'Eliminated?' Zeman said with a heavy frown. 'That means killed, I think?'

'Damn right! That's what it means, all right, and it's what I want. It's what Manny wants, as well.'

Zeman shook his head. 'She is very valuable, the Podolsky woman. But not when she is dead. Better to keep her alive. Then she can be sold. There are people who want her knowledge.'

'Dead!' Kravertz snapped. 'That's how we want her.'

'We will catch her,' Zeman said, shaking his head again. 'Then we will see who will pay the most for her.'

Kravertz glowered at him. 'What I want is also what Manny wants, and he is the boss of both of us.'

'No, no! He is important, yes. And for you, perhaps the only boss. But I have other bosses also. Maybe one of them will pay more than Manny.'

Kravertz felt the rage mounting, and the urge to tell this creature what he thought of him was almost overwhelming. The perfect situation! And this cretin was intent on destroying the best opportunity he'd ever had for resolving all his problems in one go.

Only a none-too-subtle jab in the ribs from Jed Smith stopped him in his tracks. The wake-up shot from Jed was right, Kravertz knew. They were heavily outnumbered here. And they needed Zeman and his men, if anything at all was to be achieved.

He spun round, waved his arms with frustration and said, 'OK, Milan. You win. We'll do it your way. But let's get on with it. Let's get it done!'

'Agreed,' Zeman said promptly. 'I am pleased we see it the same way now.'

Oh, no we don't, my friend! Kravertz thought. *But you can have it your way for now, at least.*

'OK with you, Jed?' he asked.

Smith nodded. 'Let's just get on with it.'

* * *

The plan they worked out was straightforward. They would attack and kill everybody inside the house except — according to Zeman — the Podolsky woman. After that, Kravertz and Smith would depart for Vaclav Havel Airport, and home.

Kravertz had no interest in the IT equipment that might be found in the house, or in seeking to destroy the Podolsky business empire either. All that was Czech, or maybe Russian, business. It would be left to Zeman, as per the agreement that had made them temporary allies.

So far as Kravertz was concerned, he would be happy to see an end to Burke, and the woman at least taken off the board as a player, so she couldn't interfere with what they had planned in the North Sea. He wouldn't object, though, if she later ended up as dead as Burke. If she survived, which was unlikely, he could always tell Manny that his own Czech allies were the reason. He and Smith had done their best.

That was the plan.

CHAPTER FIFTY-FIVE

Olga's house

Now was the time, I decided, to look to our defences once again, and to do some extra contingency planning as well. More weapons might have been useful, although guns are not my forte and both Leon and Olga knew that. I'm disinclined to use them except in exceptional circumstances, experience telling me they tend to lead to more deaths and injuries. I prefer to rely on planning, intelligence and cunning. Sometimes, though, that's not enough.

Right now, I had the Glock that Charles had given me in Prague, but that was all we had between us at the moment. I would have liked Jamie, a trained soldier, to have a gun. Bare fists have their limitations when it comes to standing up to crime gangs on foreign soil, where firearms are more plentiful, and the customs and laws are different.

'Are there any guns in the house?' I asked Olga.

She shook her head. 'Sorry, Frank. Leon wanted to leave me one but I said no, I didn't want it.'

'I understand, and that's OK. I have a gun that Charles gave me in Prague. I should let Jamie have it. As an ex-soldier, he'll be more use with it than I am.'

I headed for the door to look for him. 'Try not to worry,' I said over my shoulder. 'All this might not come to anything anyway.'

'I'm not worried, Frank,' she said with a smile.

I didn't think she was, either. I had seen her before in really dire circumstances and she hadn't been worried then, either. She just wasn't the worrying kind.

* * *

Jamie insisted he was all right and took the first watch that night, as scheduled. I was well tired, but adrenaline was coursing around my body, making deep sleep unlikely. I could manage only short bursts of unconsciousness. There was too much at stake and the situation seemed to have become quite perilous now.

I wondered if the attempt to abduct Jamie had been a one-off, a random criminal incident, or a harbinger of things to come? I just didn't know, and I didn't have Olga's equanimity. How she could have lived here alone for so long, with everything going on in her world, was beyond me. I was no Podolsky.

So I was worried, but I didn't think I would be the only one. With the government-inspired investigation continuing to make progress, even if charges and a trial were not imminent, time was fast running out for KOSC and Kravertz. No business company can withstand the kind of adverse publicity that rumours of legal action against it by the government can cause. I wondered how Jamie's old boss was coping with it all.

Time was also running out on Leon's job in the North Sea, with Olga still having nothing to show for all her work. Well into December now. Not long to go. I could see the tension in Olga, and felt sure Leon would be feeling it too.

And now this, here, in Kámen.

I had a sense that events were conspiring to come together and produce a Big Bang, with no certainty of outcome. It was deeply worrying, and not only for me.

* * *

Then things got worse. They came for us that night.

They came with deadly intent, and my fitful sleeping turned out to be a good thing. In the small hours, one of the sensors came alive with an urgent buzzing, and me with it.

I scrambled out of bed and made my way to the window overlooking the front of the house. In the desultory light from a couple of distant ancient streetlamps at this end of the village, I could see nothing that shouldn't be there. How I wished Olga had agreed to having security lights around the house.

Nor could I see anything from the window in the corridor that looked out on the back of the house. Yet the alarm was pulsing with urgent insistency. Something, or someone, had encroached on our territory. That couldn't be ignored.

I tapped lightly on the door of Olga's room, opened it and made my way over to her bed. There was no need to shake her shoulder. She had also been woken by the alarm and was sitting up.

'Something is out there,' I said quietly. 'I don't know what it is, but get ready. We may have to go.'

She nodded.

I made my way back into the corridor, dimly lit now with emergency lighting. Jamie joined me.

'Is this it?' he asked calmly.

I shrugged. 'Maybe.'

'I couldn't see anything,' he added.

'Me neither. I need to have a look outside.'

That was when we heard someone — multiple people, more like — breaking into the house. They were not bothering to be quiet about it, either. I heard timber splintering as the heavy front door was smashed open with something big and heavy being used as a battering ram.

That put an end to thoughts of foxes and wild boars, and of going outside to have a look. We knew for sure now that we were under attack.

CHAPTER FIFTY-SIX

Olga was out of her room by then, complete with her emergency bag. She looked at me questioningly. I grimaced and nodded. Then we got moving. We had rehearsed this, and we all knew what we had to do.

I dashed along the corridor to guard the top of the staircase, leaving Olga and Jamie to raise the ladder and open the trapdoor in the ceiling.

I switched the downstairs lights on from my position at the top of the stairs and risked a glance down below, spotting several milling bodies. One of them saw me and fired a quick burst from an automatic weapon that shattered the wall panelling around me and filled the air with sawdust and splinters of wood.

I ducked, withdrew for a moment and then returned fire with the Glock pistol, which I hadn't got round to giving to Jamie yet. It was totally inadequate given what we were up against, and I had no idea if I hit anyone, but returning fire served a warning and won vital seconds.

Glancing behind me, I saw the ladder was in place. Olga and Jamie were already up and out of sight, along with our emergency bags. I switched the lights off and scrambled back along the corridor to climb into the loft.

Jamie pulled the ladder up after me. Olga closed the trapdoor. Then, together, we pushed a heavy crate over it. For good measure, I grabbed a sack of cement and put that on top of the crate. Jamie added another. Even if the attackers realised where we'd gone, they would struggle to follow us.

'No lights, remember!' I whispered to the others.

'No lights are possible now,' Olga said. 'I started the countdown after hearing gunfire, and the entire electrical system will be fused by now.'

Countdown. I'd forgotten about that. It was a good thing one of us had kept it in mind.

'Well done!'

'How long have we got?' Jamie asked quietly.

'Seven minutes,' Olga replied, calm as you like.

Seven minutes only! And one or two of them gone already.

'Let's get moving!' I snapped.

Using the beam of a small torch put in place earlier, I led the way to the window at the far end of the loft. I would have preferred to show no light at all, but finding our way in total blackness would have been too much of a challenge up here given the time constraint.

Seven minutes was no time at all. Not when you considered what we had to do before those minutes were up. Nor when you winced at the gunfire and general commotion downstairs. God knows what they were shooting at. Shadows, probably. Either that, or they were wasting their time and bullets on trying to get through the steel door into the computer room.

We reached the little window at the far end of the loft. In advance, I had removed the window from its frame and covered the gap with a thin plywood board taped into place. Now I tore the board off, laid it aside and peered out into the night.

There was nothing to be seen, and all the noise was coming from below and behind us. I climbed out onto the sloping roof of the porch that adjoined that end of the house and turned to give Olga a hand. She didn't need it. Despite appearances, she was pretty nimble and was already lowering herself down to join me. Jamie followed.

We knew what we were doing, and knew we needed to crack on fast. Next, we had to reach the ground. I slid down the damp, moss-covered slates of the porch roof, and paused for a moment to check below and for the others to catch up.

The way ahead looked clear. Holding on to the heavy iron gutter, I lowered my legs over the edge of the roof and hung full-length. Then I dropped the remaining few feet to the ground. It was shrouded in darkness, which meant my landing was ungainly, but it was without damage.

I straightened up and turned to watch anxiously as Olga copied my manoeuvre and dropped to the ground. As she landed, I reached out to keep her steady and upright. We couldn't afford a sprained ankle or broken leg.

Jamie followed, without difficulty and seemingly with more ease than either Olga or me. After all the training he'd had in the army, I should have let him lead the way.

The first stage of the exit plan had now been completed, but there was no time to stand back and congratulate ourselves. The clock was ticking, and didn't have long to go. Two or three minutes now, at most, I reckoned. We set off for a nearby line of shrubs and bushes, and beyond that the forest.

CHAPTER FIFTY-SEVEN

The plan was to circle round until we could cross the road, reach the village shop and then get the Skoda out of the garage behind it. After that we would head out, probably back to Prague. The plan didn't work out. We were spotted as we crossed the open ground heading towards the forest. There were shouts and the beam from a powerful lamp caught us.

'Keep going!' I yelled at the others.

We reached the tree line without the hail of bullets I had expected coming our way. I paused, breathing heavily, and looked back. Men were starting to follow us.

'All right?' I gasped at Olga.

She nodded.

'Jamie?'

'I'm OK, Frank.'

'Right. We'll try to lose them in the forest.'

There was no point saying more. They could both see the situation as well as I could. There was no possibility of reaching the car now. We had run out of the only plan we'd had. Now we just had to keep going, and hope to stay ahead.

'You two go on,' Jamie gasped. 'Let me have the gun, Frank. I'll stay here and hold them off.'

I shook my head. 'We stay together,' I said, handing over the Glock.

Jamie might be a trained and experienced soldier, but he couldn't hold them up for long with a pistol. And then he would be dead, and so would we, soon afterwards, in all probability.

'I know this forest,' Olga said decisively. 'Come — this way!'

Jamie and I followed her as she got going.

Olga knew the forest? Well, of course she did. She'd been here a year longer than me. It would be very surprising if she hadn't explored her own backyard.

We hadn't gone more than a few yards before things changed, bringing us to a stop again. By then, in our hectic scramble, Olga's seven-minute countdown had almost been forgotten. Now it came vividly back to mind with a powerful explosion that lit up the night sky and rolled around us like thunder. I stopped, spun round and saw that the old house was bathed in light — firelight!

'Oh, my God!' I couldn't help saying it, staring at the awesome sight.

The flames changed colour and the house changed shape even as we watched.

'What did you do?' I demanded incredulously.

'We used Semtex.'

'Semtex? You had some?'

'Yes. Vladimir and the construction team brought it. Leon thought we might want some when building the tunnel.'

I just shook my head, awestruck.

Semtex, the Czech-invented plastic explosive. I was astonished Olga had known what to do with it. But I shouldn't have been. I was realising more and more that, appearance and her personal inclinations aside, Olga was just as much a warrior as the rest of the Podolsky family. She had to be. She wouldn't have survived this long otherwise.

'Come on!' I snapped, coming out of it. 'There's noth-ing here for us now.'

My thinking was that having been denied the contents of the house, the attack squad would be more eager than ever to catch up with us. If they were Russians, as I suspected, they couldn't afford total failure, not if they ever wanted to go back home again.

CHAPTER FIFTY-EIGHT

As we set off again, gunfire pursued us, and what I assumed were bullets occasionally whispered through the trees all around. They were not too close, but it was a dangerous situation. Making matters worse, it was a very dark night and the ground beneath our feet was uneven and unseen. Progress was slow. Jamie staggered heavily at one point.

'All right?' I queried over my shoulder.

'Yeah,' he gasped. 'They have no idea what they're doing. Just firing blind.'

I agreed, but random firing didn't seem to make it much less dangerous. I yearned to be deeper into the forest. That might not have been much safer in reality, but it felt like it would be. Better than the edge of the forest anyway.

Olga probably thought the same way. She led us at a good pace once we got going and into the rhythm of it. When we reached a broad track, we started jogging for a while. Soon, though, she led us off onto another very narrow path and progress slowed again.

How she managed to navigate, I had no idea. I could see almost nothing in the darkness. But she seemed to know where she was and I was happy to follow her.

Eventually, we were reduced to slow walking on a path thick with tree roots and brushwood that tripped and grabbed at us at every step. Stumbling, I should say, rather than walking. But Olga still seemed to know where we were and pressed on without hesitation. I had no idea. Increasingly, I began to wonder if she had a destination in mind or if we were just running.

We switched paths several more times. The sound of gunfire faded, and eventually stopped altogether. Long before then, all other sounds of pursuit had ceased as well, and I was confident now that no one was close behind us.

Olga came to a stop, giving us the chance to discuss what was on my mind.

'Where are we going?' I asked. 'Do you have somewhere in mind, Olga?'

'Towards the Labe canyon, and the port.'

'The port?'

That sounded so unlikely that I even wondered if it had all been too much for her, and she was hallucinating, fantasising. We had to be more than six or seven hundred miles from the sea.

'Yes,' she said. 'The port for the barges on the river. But I must call Leon now.'

She pulled out her phone and made the call. I didn't expect there to be server coverage here, but seemingly there was. I turned to Jamie as Olga began speaking in what sounded like Russian, or perhaps Ukrainian. Something that didn't sound like Czech, anyway.

'A port?' he said, sounding as puzzled as I had been.

'It's a big river, Jamie. Plenty of barge traffic going to and from Hamburg. I hadn't thought of that. You OK, by the way?'

He nodded, but he seemed a bit shaky. Not surprisingly. Shock can do that, take you that way. It had been a tough hour, or however long it had been since the sensors started buzzing.

'This won't be what you expected when you signed up with us?' I suggested, trying to be light-hearted about the situation.

'No,' he said with a wry chuckle, 'although I didn't really know what to expect. I'm OK, though. I can manage.'

'Good man!'

I turned back to Olga, who had finished speaking and was putting away her phone.

'Leon says to make for the river, but not the port. He thinks it will be too risky to go there. They could be waiting for us. Instead, he wants us to make for a ferry landing not far away. He will arrange for one of our barges to collect us from there.'

'Oh! You have a barge, and it's here?' I asked with astonishment.

'Nearby. We have a number of barges. There is much trade on the Labe.'

'What's that, the Labe?' Jamie queried.

'The river we know as the Elbe,' I told him, feeling pleased I could at least tell him something.

'The one that goes to Hamburg?'

'That's the one. Past there, actually. Another hundred miles after that it reaches the sea.'

We got moving again.

* * *

I won't pretend it was easy going after that. We were on narrow, little-trodden paths in deep coniferous forest. And it was night, and very dark. Olga went wrong a few times now, but she always managed to recover and get us back on track.

At one point she stopped and brought out her phone again, which was vibrating. Glancing at the screen, she said, 'My brother.'

There followed some incisive information deliveries, to which Olga gave brief responses, mostly affirmative.

Afterwards, she explained, 'Leon says that the barge is coming from Germany. It will stop at the landing at Dolni Zleb for us.'

'Then what?' I asked.

'Leon said he will make further plans, and let us know. Come! We must go now. The barge will reach Dolni Zleb in two or three hours. We must hurry, if we are to meet it.'

CHAPTER FIFTY-NINE

The light was improving by the time we reached the edge of
the forest and started making our way down into the Labe
canyon from the heights above Loubi. The going wasn't too
bad by then, either. We were following a well-trodden path
down through thinning woodland strewn with huge sand-
stone rocks. Down we went, through early-morning gloom,
into the depths of the canyon.

Loubi wasn't much of a port. It seemed to be more of an
industrial village on the riverside. But it was lit up by flood-
lights and there was work going on there. They were loading,
or unloading, what looked like industrial waste — piles of scrap
metal — to or from railway wagons and a couple of big barges.

I could see why Leon's advice had been to avoid Loubi.
There might well be people here waiting for us. It was a natural reception area for fugitives fleeing from the forest: bright
lights, people, houses, business premises, things happening —
and the possibility of finding help. In other circumstances, all
of that might well have attracted us. As it was, we kept well
clear.

We skirted the edge of Loubi, staying in woodland until
we were past it. Then we took to the road and headed towards
the border with Germany, which was about ten miles away,
just past the small town of Hřensko. We weren't going that

far, though. Our destination, Dolni Zleb, was only three miles or so along the road.

I say "only", but soon it became clear that that was the wrong word to use. Jamie was struggling badly. It hadn't been obvious until now, our pace through the forest necessarily being very slow due to poor light and small paths lined with tangled brushwood. But out on an open tarmac road it was. Olga and I stepped the pace up, but Jamie just couldn't cope. After a very short distance, he came to a stop.

'You go on!' he urged, when I turned to see what the problem was. 'Get Olga to safety. I'll take my chances.'

I was alarmed. 'What's wrong?' I asked, taking him by the arm.

'I got hit,' he said through gritted teeth. 'In the leg.'

Ah!

'You should have said!'

'How would that have helped?' he demanded.

Fair point. I steered him to the edge of the road, on to a patch of grass and got him sat down. Then I fished out my little torch. The beam from it made me wince even harder. There was a lot of bleeding going on. How the hell had he managed to walk this far?

'What is it?' Olga asked, coming back to join us.

'Jamie took a bullet,' I said bluntly. 'But he didn't want us to know.'

'Oh, Jamie!' Olga exclaimed. 'You should have said something.'

'Sorry,' he said, apologetic.

I was sure he was apologising more for being wounded than for not telling us. Using my pocket knife, I slit his trouser leg open. Then I grimaced and swallowed hard. His leg was a mess. We needed to stop the blood leakage, even if we could do nothing else.

'Use this,' Olga said, sizing up the situation and handing me her scarf. 'Make a . . . a tourniquet?'

'That's the word,' I said grimly, taking the scarf. 'Thank you.'

Once again, I thought, Olga had come to the rescue. It was pretty damned ironic really. We were supposed to be looking after her.

I did the best I could with the scarf. Then I gave Jamie a couple of painkillers from a packet I had, along with a sip of water from my bottle. The pain was obviously getting to him now, which wasn't surprising, but we still had some distance to go. He was going to have to do his best to hang in there and keep going. We couldn't leave him, and we couldn't carry him.

We got him to his feet. With Olga and me supporting him on either side, we began to hobble on towards our destination. By then, I was working out in my head how far we had to go, how long it would take us, what to do if we couldn't make the rendezvous, and a bunch of other stuff. There were an awful lot of unknowns in that calculation. Too many. I gave up. We would just have to do the best we could. Then I had a better idea.

'Olga, is it possible for you to contact the barge skipper?'

'I can try. Leon said he would send me his phone number.'

'Good. Don't bother now, but perhaps you can try in a little while, when we stop for a rest.'

I was thinking of asking the skipper if he could slow down, to give us more time to reach the pick-up place. I knew there was no point asking to be picked up where we were. He would need a jetty to make a landing. No way would he risk grounding his barge in soft mud at the edge of the river, or grinding against a rocky crag.

'Leave me,' Jamie muttered. 'You go on.'

'No way!' I told him sharply.

I still hoped it wouldn't come to that, but increasingly I was thinking that it might well. Game as he was, Jamie was in a lot of trouble.

A big wagon appeared ahead of us, roaring down the long road into Děčín from Germany. I steered us off the road and into the trees, just in case it was our friends from Kámen, coming to see if we had made it this far. Then we sat Jamie down and I asked Olga to try to make contact with the barge.

CHAPTER SIXTY

It took her a while, but Olga managed to make contact with the barge skipper. Leon had already spoken to him. So he knew the score, knew what was expected of him. As I had thought, he couldn't pick us up from the riverbank. He needed the assurance of a solid landing to tie up to. The ferry landing at Dolni Zleb was the nearest place offering that. We would just have to struggle on and get there.

More positively, he understood the problem we had. To help, he would have an engine problem when he reached Dolni Zleb, and be obliged to wait there until the engine was fixed — meaning, when we arrived.

So we had every incentive to struggle on further, and we bent ourselves to the task with gritted teeth. I have to say Olga was wonderful. She was the one we were supposed to be protecting and saving, but the reality now was that she was doing her full share of helping me haul Jamie to safety.

Alone, I doubt I could have got him there, especially as his condition deteriorated. Pain, blood loss, painkillers all combined to make him a wreck. Eventually, he couldn't walk any more at all. We ended up carrying him short distances at a time. Somehow — God knows how! — we got there.

It was full daylight well before we arrived, and the skipper had a man ashore waiting for us. As soon as he saw us in the distance, he called to a colleague. Then they both ran along the road to help, and ended up carrying Jamie the last quarter mile between them.

Jamie was got aboard, and into a bunk bed in one of the crew cabins. Olga spoke at some length to the skipper while that was going on. Then she introduced me to him. We shook hands and he gave me a friendly nod and smile before turning away to start ringing bells and pressing buttons. With a roar, the mighty engines miraculously recovered and the barge began to manoeuvre back out into mid-stream.

I had never been aboard a vessel like that before. My sole experience of life on an inland waterway had been aboard a narrowboat on a canal somewhere in the English Midlands. That had been a picturesque and slow way of travelling, even though we were powered by an engine rather than a horse. This was very different. And impressive.

The Podolsky barge had wonderful accommodation for the crew: separate cabins, galley kitchen, lounge equipped with the entertainment facilities to be found in a top-class hotel. And it had an engine room equipped with a massive Volvo engine that powered mighty pistons. It was a barge, Olga told me, that could comfortably undertake sea journeys as well as navigate the rivers and canals across Europe.

I was also told that the journey to Hamburg usually took only half the week or two needed for the return leg, and sometimes, when the river was in flood, much less than that. Travelling upstream, against the current, which we were doing, though, was always a slower, more stately process. Regardless, as usual the big engine did what it was called on to do, and the Podolsky barge coped magnificently. In an hour or so, we were passing by the main port in Děčín, where many barges were in dock for loading and unloading, and presumably for maintenance as well.

Our barge's journey was to terminate at Ústí nad Labem, a big industrial town some twenty miles further on. But long before we got there, we slowed to little more than a holding position in mid-stream. I watched with fascination as a helicopter arrived overhead and began to make a gentle descent until it landed on the deck of the barge. Even before I saw her, I didn't have any doubt who the pilot was. Lenka was putting in a good shift once again.

Events moved fast after that. Paramedics emerged to take charge of Jamie and get him aboard the chopper on a stretcher. After shaking the hand of the skipper, Olga and I followed. It was very like the efficient medical mission that had taken Charles off the battlefield in Prague, and I have to say I was grateful to be in the hands of the Podolsky machine once again.

Leon was waiting for us aboard the chopper. That wasn't a surprise, either. I assumed he needed to see with his own eyes that Olga was safe. Perhaps me, too. And I had little doubt that he was also very anxious to quiz Jamie on what he knew about KOSC. Those of us who had been fighting for our lives in Kámen might have pushed all that aside, but I didn't doubt for a moment that Leon wouldn't have.

He and I grinned and shook hands. He hugged Olga. Then the chopper lifted and we set off. We were heading for Prague, I read from Olga's lips above the clatter of the engine. Of course we were. In this country, all roads seemed to lead to Prague.

CHAPTER SIXTY-ONE

Podolsky Medical Centre, Prague
10 December

Once again, Lenka landed the chopper on top of the medical centre. There wasn't quite the same urgency with Jamie as there had been with Charles, but as before, the patient was quickly and efficiently carried away into the depths of the building, there to be tended to by medics who must have been well accustomed to dealing with gunshot wounds.

Olga and I followed Leon at a more leisurely pace and took a small elevator that transported us to what I regarded as Leon's bachelor suite. By now, I knew that to be a misnomer. Leon was actually a loyal family man, and far too busy to spend time philandering. "Guest accommodation" was a better description of the rooms, but bachelor pad was how it had looked to me when I first stayed there.

It was a very well-equipped bachelor pad, too, and even more so now. A computer room stacked with equipment had been added since my previous visit. My eyes glazed over, and my heart sank, when I saw it all. Not so Olga, though. She excused herself and dived inside after a rapid exchange with

Leon that sounded to be all about business. I assumed that despite the excesses of the past night, and notwithstanding fatigue and shock, she wanted to get back to work. How could I ever have thought her a timid, sensitive soul?

Leon and I left her to it and retired to the living area, and the kitchen. My host got to work with a coffee maker. I left him to it and went to look out of the window at the street scene far below. For the moment, at least, there was nothing better for me to do. The respite was very welcome, but I suspected it wouldn't last long.

'Coffee, Frank?'

I turned and nodded. 'Make it a strong one. A shot of caffeine is just what I need at the moment.'

'You had a rough night,' he said. 'And you did well — you and Mr Burke. I will thank you now, and Jamie in person once the doctors have finished with him.'

'I don't know how well we did, Leon. Olga's house was destroyed, and all that equipment lost, your timetable threatened, and Olga herself vastly inconvenienced.'

'But you saved her. That is what matters most. And that is why I wanted you here. I won't pretend the rest doesn't matter, but you know how we feel about Olga.'

I nodded. He was right, of course. I just didn't like the idea that we had had to run and implement a scorched earth policy. Men may well have died back there, too. Not our men, but human beings all the same. Things could have gone better. They probably would have done, had Vladimir and his construction crew stayed with us.

'We were outnumbered and out-gunned, Leon. Olga needs better protection than Jamie and I were able to give her.'

'We all make choices in this life, Frank. And that includes Olga. Risk inevitably accompanies our choices.'

I smiled ruefully. 'Ever the philosopher, Leon! But you're right. I'm just not very happy at the moment. I'll get over it.'

'I hope you do,' Leon said, with a serious look. 'There is much to do.'

* * *

We sat and drank coffee for a few minutes, and waited for a call that would let us know the medics had finished their work and it would be convenient for Jamie to be visited. The subject of the deadline Leon was working towards also came up. There wasn't long to go now. Six days, I reckoned. Not long at all.

'Has Olga found anything yet?' I asked. 'Any signs of interference with pipelines?'

Leon shook his head. 'No. And we have only six more days. That is why she has gone back to work immediately.'

'And she can do that from here?'

'Oh, yes. It is almost the same here as in Kámen. She has what she needs, even if here is not where she would choose to be.'

Other places, too, I was thinking. Not only Kámen. The work would be possible elsewhere, as well as here and there. Genuine distance working. It was very impressive, in its way, to me at least. But, then, I'm not a functioning part of the IT world. I'm just a bystander.

Leon answered a buzz on his phone, listened and gave a brief reply.

'We can see Jamie,' he told me. 'They have repaired the damage for now. I am told he is weak from blood loss and sedation, but otherwise he is in good shape. He's a pretty tough guy, I would say.'

I agreed. Jamie had walked a long way with a bullet-holed leg, and never once complained or felt sorry for himself. He had simply walked until he could walk no further.

'A good man, as well as a tough one,' I said.

CHAPTER SIXTY-TWO

We called in to see Olga before we visited Jamie.

'Not good,' she said in English, in response to her brother's burst of Slavonic language. 'I have nothing to report.'

They were both tense, anxious even. I could see that. Leon was like a caged lion at the best of times; now, he was vibrating with the tension. His calm exterior appearance didn't fool me. The man was more stressed than I'd ever seen him.

Olga, too. She was more upset about not finding anything on the pipelines she was monitoring than about the loss of her house and our mad flight from Kámen.

Leon rattled away at her again. She shrugged and threw up her arms with exasperation.

'I am telling her to get some rest,' Leon said.

It was good advice.

'How important, at the end of the day, is this project?' I asked, eager to introduce a sense of proportion and calm things down a bit.

'For us Podolskys, not very,' Leon said sharply. 'If we fail, we may lose some credibility, but we can cope with that. But for your country, it is extremely important.

'Assuming the intelligence is right, which we believe it is, in a very short time there will be a massive explosion that could send a tsunami of oil washing across the North Sea and the coast of the eastern seaboard of the UK. It will also cause big energy supply problems and demonstrate to the world that your government is incapable of protecting the nation's vital infrastructure.

'If it is a gas pipeline, the cost for energy supply and government credibility will still be high, but pollution will not be so great. Possibly only the fishing industry will be affected, with the loss of much marine life.'

Leon stopped and shrugged. Then he rubbed his face with his hands and yawned. He was tired, too, as well as everything else he was. A lot was resting on Podolsky shoulders.

The situation was very worrying indeed. Leon was agitated about the possibility of failure, but my own distress was more personal. It was my coast and my part of the North Sea that was going to be hit hardest if disaster occurred. The consequences could be even greater than those Leon had summarised.

Even so, no good could come of allowing Olga to drive herself into the ground. She had to be close to exhaustion. Realistically, given that she had found nothing yet, how likely was it that she would in the time remaining? Some rest might help.

'As I understand it, Leon,' I said, 'your sea drones are getting on with their work almost independently. Anything they find will be logged and analysed, and their work will continue until they are ready to be collected. So why not just let them get on with it, or have someone else monitor them, and let Olga get some sleep?'

Olga made noises indicating dissent, but Leon nodded. 'You're right, Frank. Come on, Olga! You've been through enough for one day. Give it a rest. Don't make me shut down the power to the building and force you to rest.'

She began to argue. Then she shut up. Perhaps she accepted that if the world was going to hell in a handcart, it wouldn't all be down to her.

'It is true,' she admitted, finding the serene persona I associated with her. 'I am tired. I must sleep, and recover. First, though, I will ask HQ to take over and let me know immediately anything is found.'

HQ, eh? Where was that, I wondered? Switzerland? Or Samphire Batts, the Podolsky Teesside base? But I wasn't going to ask.

We left Olga and went to see Jamie.

CHAPTER SIXTY-THREE

Jamie was lying in bed, unmoving and linked to tubes dangling from an overhead gantry, for want of a better word for the apparatus. He looked sleepy, no doubt because of sedatives and painkillers, and whatever else he'd been given. Our overnight exertions must have had a part to play, as well. I was feeling out of sorts myself. It was only Leon's boundless energy, and positivism radiating from him in waves, that was keeping me going at the moment.

'How are you doing, Jamie?' I asked.

'Good,' he said, stirring himself and speaking with a slow, growly voice. 'Never better. You?'

I had to smile. Never better! What was he like? His career in the ring, or in the army, must have taught him always to look on the bright side of life.

'Probably not as good as you, mate!' I told him. 'They treating you well here?'

'Great! Some nice people.'

'That's good. Leon's come with me, Jamie. We wanted to see how you were doing, and he wants to talk to you about the problem he has. Do you feel up to it?'

'Right as rain,' he said slowly, forcing himself up through the fog enveloping him.

I nodded to Leon and stepped back. Jamie wasn't in great shape, but I was confident he would do his best.

Leon took it easy with him, speaking gently and slowly, telling him how much he appreciated what he had done, and how sorry he was that he had suffered so much. Jamie didn't have the strength to do much more than listen, but he did that very well. After a minute or two, Leon cut to the chase and spoke of KOSC.

'Even before I knew of your troubles, Jamie, I had heard of your old employer and his company. He's not a good man, as you came to realise for yourself. For some time, the British authorities have been investigating his company, for various reasons. Possible illegal activity concerning finance and how the company is run, tax evasion and so on.'

'Investigation?' Jamie murmured. 'I know. Everybody knows.'

'Probably. But very recently, the authorities have learned of things much more serious. KOSC seem to be involved in a conspiracy to sabotage vital infrastructure under the North Sea. Do you know anything about that, Jamie?'

I watched Jamie's face as he struggled to force himself to stay awake.

'Yes,' he said. 'It is why the divers were . . . were murdered, and why . . .'

'And why you have been on the run,' Leon said. 'I understand that, Jamie. What else do you know? What can you tell Frank and me about it?'

Not much, it seemed. Jamie only wanted to talk about the murdered divers. Perhaps it was all he knew, and certainly what mattered most to him personally. He had been living with the consequences for many months.

'Oil and gas from under the North Sea are important to Britain,' Leon pressed gently. 'You know that.'

'Yes. Very . . .'

'If the supply is stopped or interrupted, there will be big problems.'

'Big problems, yes.'

'That is why the Admiralty asked us to help monitor the pipelines, looking for things that should not be there. Explosives, they think.'

Jamie shook his head from side to side slowly, and looked a bit puzzled.

'That is what Olga has been doing, using the drones,' Leon pressed. 'It is why her work is so important, and why you and Frank have been brought here to protect her.

'The Admiralty asked us to help them search for things like that because we have done it successfully in other places, like the Red Sea and the Persian Gulf. We have a lot of experience. But we are running out of time now, Jamie. In just a few days something terrible is likely to happen. A big explosion, and much oil everywhere, and . . .'

Jamie's head was still shaking. Leon stepped back and looked at me with a shrug and a despairing expression. 'It's no good,' he said quietly. 'He doesn't hear, or understand.'

I frowned. I wasn't so sure.

'Jamie,' I said quietly, 'is there anything you can tell us?'

'Oil and gas,' he muttered.

'Oil and gas, yes?'

His head moved from side to side again. What did that mean?

'Oil and gas?' I repeated.

'No!'

Just the one word, uttered forcibly. It seemed to exhaust him. He immediately sank back into the pillows and his eyes closed. But it was as if a door had briefly opened into his mind. Leon had seen that, too. We glanced at one another. He nodded. Then he turned away, pulled out his phone and made a call.

'A doctor,' he said aside to me. 'We must wake him.'

I grimaced, but he was right. It might not be good for Jamie, but for a moment there, it had seemed that we were on the edge of something that might be very important. We couldn't just let Jamie run out on us.

I didn't really know what Leon said to the doctor who answered his call, but I could guess. He wanted Jamie revived, if only briefly. That might not be good medical practice, but we were facing an emergency, and although Jamie was not in great shape, his life was not in danger. That was what I thought, anyway.

The doctor came to the same conclusion. He produced a syringe and gave Jamie a shot of adrenaline, or of something else that served to wake him up.

CHAPTER SIXTY-FOUR

Jamie came to once again and squinted at me, as if wondering
where he was and what was going on.

'Welcome back!' I said with a grin.

He grunted something not very sensible, but I guessed
it wasn't complimentary. At least, he was awake.

'We were asking you about oil and gas pipelines, Jamie,
remember?'

He just looked at me as if he hadn't a clue what I was
talking about.

'What Kravertz was doing, and KOSC, to oil and gas
pipelines. You kept saying "no" to something. What was it?'

He hesitated a few moments, as if uncertain. Then he
cleared his throat and said, 'Not them, no.'

'What do you mean?'

'Not oil and gas pipelines. Not them. That wasn't it.'

I was mystified. Jamie sighed heavily, as if we were wasting his time. He wanted to go back to sleep.

'What, then?' I prompted.

He struggled to get the words together, but they came
eventually.

'Cable,' he said gruffly.

I was even more puzzled. 'What do you mean?'

'Not pipelines,' he said, shaking his head slowly from side to side. 'Big cable.'

'Cable? What sort of cable?'

'Electric.'

'Power cable, you mean? From a windfarm?'

'Not that, no.' Jamie shook his head again. 'Soon. Ready soon.'

Now truly mystified, I stepped back and turned to Leon, but he was already gone. All I saw of him was a glimpse of his back as the door swung shut after him.

And when I turned back to Jamie, he was gone, too.

The doctor, who had stayed after giving the injection that had brought him round briefly, said, 'Enough, I think. I will not give him more. It would be too dangerous.'

I just nodded. 'Thank you for your help, Doctor.'

CHAPTER SIXTY-FIVE

Things moved pretty fast after that, not that they ever went slowly around the Podolskys. My head was buzzing as I looked for Leon. I wondered what he had made of Jamie's mutterings.

Leon wasn't in the apartment. Not in the residential part of it, at least. But I found him and Olga both in the computer room. They were very busy. Leon was on the phone, having an agitated conversation with someone who seemed to be being difficult. Olga was racing between screens and keypads, phones and printers. There was a lot of noise and flashing lights.

I guessed it all had to do with what Jamie had just said. A chord had been struck. Leon glanced round when his call ended, saw me and beckoned me to a quieter corner of the room.

'What's going on?' I asked him.

'A reset, a total reset.'

'Because of what Jamie said?'

'Yes. You heard him. It's nothing to do with the pipe-lines we've been monitoring. No wonder Olga hasn't been able to find anything. The Admiralty got it wrong.'

I nodded. That was certainly what it seemed like, always assuming Jamie knew what he was talking about.

'Do you know anything about a new cable, Leon?'

'I can't be sure, but I'm assuming he was talking about a new interconnector. That's a big cable that transfers electricity between countries.'

He looked at me expectantly. I just shrugged. It meant nothing to me.

'OK, Frank. I'm ahead of you. A new one has been built between Norway and the UK. It comes ashore at Teesmouth, just a couple of miles from our place at Samphire Batts.'

Ah!

'And it's nearly complete?'

'It is complete. In a couple of days there will be a big celebration, and a massive publicity launch for it.

'After what Jamie said, I believe that cable, or the celebration of it, is what is being targeted. It's nothing to do with pipelines, or oil and gas.'

'So Olga is . . . ?'

'Re-routing the drones, restarting the processes. And I must alert the Admiralty to this change. They may disagree, and want me to continue doing what we've been doing, but the hell with that! Jamie has cracked it for us.'

He excused himself and rushed off to make phone calls. I watched Olga for a while, but there was nothing I could do there. I was in danger of being in the way.

All I could do for the moment was summon up everything I knew about subsea cables, and review what I knew. That took me all of three seconds. Then I retreated to the medical department to keep Jamie company while he slept. At least I could do that.

CHAPTER SIXTY-SIX

Jamie was out of it. I let him be. He had earned a rest. So had I, actually. It had been a tough twenty-four hours, even if I hadn't been shot, wounded and lost a lot of blood. So I sank wearily into a bedside chair in Jamie's room and tried to relax.

I didn't want to go over things anymore, but I couldn't help doing it. This thing that Jamie and I had found ourselves involved in was a whole lot bigger than the job I had signed up for. Guarding Olga in a remote rural retreat in Northern Bohemia was a long way removed from protecting a new and vital part of the UK's energy supply system from a desperate and violent gang of criminals intent on sabotaging it and murdering anyone in their way!

It was also a long way from a seemingly iffy offshore company based on the north bank of the Tees. Yet that same company, long a threat to Jamie Burke, was also represented here in Northern Bohemia, strange as that seemed until you worked through it. The explanation was simple, straightforward even, once you had done that.

Both Jamie Burke and Olga Podolsky had to be eliminated if KOSC was to be successful both in surviving investigation and sabotaging the new cable between the UK and

Norway. That was the truth of it. And that was what had brought Daniel Kravertz and his acolytes and cronies to the Czech Republic, where both Jamie and Olga were conveniently located.

Whether or not they had known Jamie was here was a question impossible for me to answer. They might have. Alternatively, it could just have been a happy coincidence for them to find him here, when what they had come for was Olga, the heart of the Podolsky project.

Having reached that conclusion, I shook my head and let my mind wander a bit. That was a mistake. Pretty soon it came up with some questions that had been brushed under the carpet for convenience.

One was the thought that Kravertz seemed to have a lot of help — local help, presumably. But who was providing it, especially at such short notice?

That raised another question: was Kravertz alone in the sabotage scheme, or was some other unknown person or organisation involved, one with a presence here in this country? If there was such a person or entity, what was Kravertz's role: partner, initiator or client?

Then, of course, I began to think about the elephant in the room: who would stand to gain from a successful attack on the cable, the interconnector? Malevolent state actor, or private criminal enterprise?

Second conclusion? I needed a lot more information if I was ever to be able to answer questions like those.

CHAPTER SIXTY-SEVEN

'How's it going?' I asked with a weary yawn, as Leon came into the room sometime later.

'Good. Olga has been re-routing the drones, and she's got them started on the new cable. An initial scan will take about ten hours. Meanwhile, I've told the Admiralty what we've learned and what we're doing about it. Given that we've found nothing so far on oil or gas pipelines in our area, they think we might be onto something. We'll see soon enough. How is Jamie, by the way?'

'Flat out, as you've seen. He needs to rest, but the doctors say he should be fine. I just thought I would get out of your way and sit with him for a while.'

'That's good. I am sorry about all this, Frank. Neither of you could have expected what you've got yourselves into.'

'Well, Jamie certainly couldn't, but I've been here with you before, Leon!'

He grinned and shook his head. Then he attempted another apology that I waved aside.

'I've been doing some thinking while I sit here,' I added. 'Who or what do you think is behind all this? Do you still not know, or have any idea, Leon?'

He blew out his cheeks and grimaced. 'Good question. I still don't know, I'm afraid. The Admiralty don't know, either. There are suspicions, of course, but the priority all along has been to stop the sabotage happening, rather than worry about who is ultimately responsible.'

That made sense. It had to be the priority. All the same . . .

'Russia, perhaps?' I said.

'Perhaps. But who in Russia? Is it an attack by the Russian state, or one of its agencies, or an attack by some person or private body? For that matter, it could be an attack by some other state, or just some private operator with no connection to Russia. We just don't know.'

'And your friends in the Admiralty can't even hazard a guess?'

'Not until they are sure, or someone else has said they are sure and have the evidence.'

'OK. That's the Admiralty, and presumably the British Government. But what do you, personally, think is most likely, Leon? You can speak freely, especially to me. People in the Admiralty probably can't.'

'Me? For me, it is a very simple process of elimination. I ask myself who will gain if this sabotage event happens. People in the Kremlin, and people in Russia's military and intelligence communities, would regard it as a successful strike against Western interests that demonstrates their power to intervene wherever they choose. But would the possibility of such a disruption be big enough to justify Russian interest? I really don't know that it would.

'On the other hand, there are people and organisations with nothing to do with Russia, or international politics, who could make money out of an event like this.'

'Really?'

'Oh, yes. Always where there is drama and emergency, someone makes money, sometimes by accident, sometimes because they planned it that way. If electricity from the inter- connector fails, the UK would have to buy electricity from elsewhere to make up the shortfall. And it would be at a short-term price, which would be higher than the price in a long-term contract.

'So even if it were only for a few days or hours, somebody would make many millions of pounds, dollars, roubles — or whatever currency they use.'

Hmm. That was something to think about.

I returned to my original question. 'But you really don't know whether this has been planned by a hostile state or just someone intent on making a lot of money?'

He shook his head. 'Sorry, Frank. I don't.'

CHAPTER SIXTY-EIGHT

The outskirts of Kámen
Early morning

Kravertz had been lucky to survive. He knew that. He also knew that if he had any sense, he wouldn't have been there himself in the first place, but he had been unable to resist the opportunity to eliminate both his and Manny's top priorities at one and the same time.

As it was, he emerged from the Podolsky house in rags and bleeding, and raging about how things had gone in there. They'd got nothing!

'You OK, boss?' Jed Smith asked.

Kravertz spat out blood and sawdust, and Christ knew what else, and nodded. He was suffering, but he knew that the three of Zeman's men who had been trying to break through the steel door to get access to the computer room would not be suffering. There was probably nothing left of them.

But that was Zeman's problem. They had been nothing to do with him. It was Zeman who had wanted to get at the computer and the machines, not him. His interest had been in Burke and the Russian woman, and now it looked like they had both got away.

He ground his teeth with frustration and pain. *Holy damn!* These burns were sore.

'What about you, Jed?' he remembered to ask. 'You OK?'

'Not even a scratch. But I wasn't inside the house.'

True. Kravertz wished now that he'd sent Jed inside, and stayed well out of it himself. 'You didn't even see Burke?'

Smith shook his head. 'It's fucking enormous, this place. I was at the back, but they didn't come that way. One of the Czechs spotted them going out the other side.'

'Bastards!' Kravertz ground his teeth again. 'Where did they go?'

'Dunno. Making for the woods, I think. But here's Zeman. Ask him.'

Kravertz turned to face the Czech boss, and shielded his face from the blaze that had erupted in the house.

'We gotta get out of here,' Zeman yelled. 'Now!'

Kravertz was reluctant to move, having come this far and got so close to his targets, but he knew Zeman was right. There was nothing they could do here now, and the explosion and the fire would be attracting a lot of interest. Probably all sorts of authority, as well, if there was any out here in this back of nowhere.

'You are hurt, my friend?' Zeman bawled at him.

'Nothing serious,' Kravertz replied. 'Just burns and scratches.'

That was enough, but he knew he'd been lucky.

'You lost men?' he said to Zeman as they jogged back to their waiting vehicles.

'Three. They were inside the house, like you. It's a pity. They were good men.'

'I left them trying to break into the basement.'

'That would be where the computer was. It was their target. What were you doing?'

'Looking for Burke, the guy we were after. And the Podolsky woman. I had Jed wait outside, at the back of the house, in case they got out that way. But he didn't see them.'

Nothing more was said until the two of them were inside the first vehicle and the driver had them hurtling down the road. The others would be following in the second vehicle.

'So they got away,' Kravertz said bitterly, unable to conceal his anger and disappointment.

'Maybe,' Zeman said.

'Only maybe?'

'I have men following them in the forest. Two are hunters. They will find them.'

'I hope so,' Kravertz said with feeling, daring to hope that maybe all was not lost after all.

CHAPTER SIXTY-NINE

Prague

I crashed out in one of the bedrooms and managed a few hours of much-needed sleep. Leon woke me the next day, while it was still dark.

'We've got it, Frank!'

'Got what?' I asked, sitting up.

'Olga has found it!'

That galvanised me. I got out of bed and grabbed my clothes.

'The interconnector?'

'Yes! Jamie was right about that. We'd been looking in the wrong place. Thank God he was here!'

'There are explosives in several places along the length of the cable, wrapped in waterproof bundles together with lithium batteries. One of them will contain the master switch that blows the whole lot up together.'

'Which one?'

'We don't know yet. Olga is talking to the Royal Navy experts about that. Meanwhile, the navy is getting dive teams in position at the various sites.'

'It's going to be touch and go,' I pointed out. 'Five days to go?'

Leon nodded.

'Jamie might be able to help with that, as well — locating the master switch,' I suggested. 'Let's see if he's awake.'

* * *

He was. Jamie was awake and alert. He grinned at us when we burst into his room.

'I've caused you more trouble than I was worth, Frank,' he said ruefully.

'Don't think that,' I told him. 'We certainly don't. How are you feeling?'

'Good. Recovered — apart from the leg.'

He was over the medication, he meant. It might be a while before he was walking again, though.

'Pleased to hear it, Jamie. Leon needs your help again.'

Leon summarised the situation, saying that, until Jamie had told them it was the interconnector that was being targeted, all Olga's efforts had been misdirected. They had wasted weeks searching oil and gas pipelines. Now they hoped he could help again.

'We believe one of the packages of explosives will contain a master switch that will detonate the whole string when it's activated. We've got to hit that first. Do you have any idea which one it might be?'

Jamie frowned and thought about it for a few moments. Then he said, 'I don't really know, but I'm pretty sure it will be the one nearest the shore.'

'So that the explosion will be seen from onshore?'

'There's that,' Jamie agreed with a nod. 'But, also, because it was the last package to be placed, and the one that the divers Kravertz shot didn't want anything to do with.'

Leon looked at me.

'It makes sense,' I said.

'I'll get back to the Royal Navy and tell them that,' Leon said decisively. 'They're handling it from now on. Thanks, Jamie! You've been a great help.'

Then Leon was gone.

Jamie looked at me and, appearing worried, said, 'I could be wrong, but . . .'

'But?'

'But I don't think I am. I think I'm right.'

'Don't worry about it,' I told him. 'They'll soon find out.'

CHAPTER SEVENTY

Prague
14 December

I didn't know if Olga had had any sleep. Probably not. She looked very tired, but she was buzzing all the same, like the rest of us, even more so when the navy go-between told Leon that the master cache of explosives had been found and de-activated, just two days before time was to run out. The interconnector was saved, and the official celebrations could go ahead as planned.

We were all absolutely jubilant by then. A great deal of back-slapping and high-fiving went on. Faces were creased in what threatened to be permanent smiles, and Leon's bachelor pad, normally so quiet and peaceful, reverberated with the whooping and hollering.

Leon decided that all of us, including the not-very-mobile Jamie, should transfer to the main Podolsky residence and celebrate properly. No one objected to that. So off we went, in a fleet of vehicles that were a big upgrade on Olga's little Skoda.

To be truthful, it was a rather quiet party when we got there. But, then, I'd never known Leon to do riotous partying. Anyway, it suited me. The mood was one of exuberant satisfaction and happy comradeship, rather than a drunken celebration in what I romantically thought of as classic, traditional Russian style. No wild music and extravagant behaviour. Nothing like that. We just enjoyed a fine meal and some even finer wine, and congratulated Olga, Jamie, IT people, and each other on a job well done.

Alone in a quiet corner, I reflected about the destruction wrought in Kámen, and wondered if the people who had organised the attack there, and the planned sabotage in the North Sea, would ever be identified and brought to justice. It seemed unlikely. Those who had survived the explosion in the old house would have scattered, and I doubted that the forces of law and order in this country would ever catch up with them, or even discover who they were.

One exception, of course, was Daniel Kravertz, Jamie's former boss. Eventually, the investigation into KOSC would bring him down, even if Kámen or the three murders Jamie had witnessed didn't. As Henry had reminded me, even Al Capone hadn't been able to withstand a tax evasion charge.

Perhaps Jed Smith, Kravertz's sidekick, would also meet justice. He seemed to be an integral part of all this, too. Maybe others would be drawn into the net eventually, as well. I had to hope so. Surely the Czech authorities would identify the local gang who had been helping Kravertz?

I also wondered about the old house, and how Olga felt about its loss. Shock and sadness, presumably, once she had calmed down from the exhilaration of finding the explosives on the interconnector. But she would recover, and deal with the loss. I was sure of that.

As if on cue, I noticed Olga discreetly withdrawing from the gathering. No doubt she was exhausted. Along with Jamie, she had been personally targeted, and she had seen her home go up in flames. She had a lot to process.

I smiled and nodded to her when she caught my eye just before leaving the room. If she felt she needed some quiet time alone, I for one didn't begrudge her seeking it. She deserved nothing but gratitude and well wishes from us all.

CHAPTER SEVENTY-ONE

Two days earlier

Zeman said they were heading back to Prague. They were done here. They had failed. 'We need to get away from here fast,' he added, 'before people come looking for us.'

Kravertz agreed, but couldn't resist asking, 'What about the guys you left in the woods, the hunters?'

Zeman didn't bother replying. His silence itself a response to such a question. An uncomfortable atmosphere developed in the vehicle. To Kravertz, it meant Zeman had given up, having decided there was nothing more he could do. That meant he and Smith had to give up, as well. There was no way they could carry on alone.

'Well,' he said, 'we'll go back to your place, Milan, and get cleaned up. Then me and Jed will look for flights back to the UK, I guess. No point staying any longer.'

He was looking for a reaction, and he got one.

'No!' Zeman said firmly. 'That is not possible.'

'Which part isn't possible?' Kravertz asked with a chuckle. 'Getting cleaned up or getting flights back to the UK?'

'Manny will not like that. You must stay here with us.'

'Have a holiday, you mean?'

'Yes, yes! Holiday.'

'Sounds lovely.'

Then Kravertz began to think things through with a clear eye.

What the hell was going on, he wondered? It sounded like they were in jail. Were they prisoners? What difference did it make to Zeman if they stayed or left for home? And what, exactly, was the link between Zeman and Manny?

It took a while, but by the time they reached Zeman's base in Prague he believed he had got hold of it. He had assembled a picture that was different to the one he had brought with him from Haverton Hill, and it wasn't one he liked. In fact, it shocked him. He needed to do some fresh thinking and planning, and he needed to take Jed into his confidence a bit more.

CHAPTER SEVENTY-TWO

It wasn't until they were back in their room at Zeman's base that Kravertz had the opportunity to speak to Smith, and level with him.

'You OK?' he asked.

'Me?' Smith shook his head. 'Not really, no. Why? What's on your mind?'

'Maybe the same thing that's on your mind, Jed. Maybe a bit more. I'm thinking the situation, our situation, isn't right. There's stuff going on here that I don't understand, and don't like.'

Smith nodded. 'I know what you mean, boss. How do you read it?'

Kravertz sighed, and shook his head.

'How I see it now, and only now, is that I don't think we're supposed to get out of here alive, either of us.'

Smith nodded thoughtfully. 'As bad as that?'

'I think it is. If so, Zeman slipped up back at that woman's house. That was the time, and place, to get rid of us easily. He didn't manage to do it. Either he didn't expect me to go inside the house, or the explosion unnerved him and upset his plan.

'I think we were supposed to end up as dead as Burke. Maybe as the woman, as well, but I'm not sure about that. He had ideas about selling her to the highest bidder.'

'I wondered what was going on,' Smith said with a grimace. 'Something I didn't tell you, boss, is that I had to take out the Czech guy I was partnered with back there.'

'Oh?'

'I tripped just as he was going to shoot me in the back. When I looked up, he had his gun levelled at me. So I kicked him in the balls and grabbed it. Then I did to him what he'd been going to do to me, and all the way back I kept hold of the gun, in case any of the others had the same idea he'd had.'

'Well done, Jed,' Kravertz said thoughtfully. 'That pretty much confirms what I was thinking. Without the explosion, I probably wouldn't have come out of that house alive either. No wonder Zeman didn't seem to know what to say on the journey back here. All his plans up shit creek!'

'Who's behind it? Is it just him?'

'No.' Kravertz shook his head. 'I don't think so. I reckon it's Manny. There's no one else it could be. Zeman has taken orders from him.'

'Manny? I thought . . .'

'Manny,' Kravertz said firmly. 'I think he's decided me and you have outlived our usefulness to him. Maybe the KOSC investigation is close to an end, now they have a murder rap to throw at us. Manny probably wants to close us down, write us off and cut his losses.

'Also, we've set the cable thing up for him, and it'll go off in a day or two. What better finale for him than to end up with that and us going down, along with Burke and the Podolsky woman?'

Smith grimaced. 'It's hard to believe.'

'It is. I agree. But it fits.'

There was silence for a few moments while they each mulled things over.

'What about the Brotherhood?' Smith asked eventually. 'Are they still behind it all?'

Kravertz shook his head. 'It's just Manny, I believe. Something you said a while ago got me thinking. Now I don't believe there is any Brotherhood. It's just been Manny spinning us a line. Especially me,' he added bitterly. 'And I fell for it.'

Smith got up slowly. 'I need a drink,' he said, heading for the minibar in a corner of the room.

'Get one for me, as well. Just one, mind, Jed! We've got some thinking to do.'

'Jim Beam OK?' Smith asked, gazing at the array of bottles. 'Sure.'

'Or Jack Daniels?'

'Now you're talking!'

'Quite a hoard in here,' Smith said, shaking his head at the array of labels.

'Don't use a bottle already open,' Kravertz warned. 'Let's not risk making it too easy for them.'

CHAPTER SEVENTY-THREE

'We can still turn this around, Jed,' Kravertz said.

'We can? What you got in mind?'

'The way I figure it, there's no point going back to Haverton Hill. That, and the whole KOSC business, is over and gone now.'

'It's that bad?'

'We've gotta be realistic, Jed. That damned investigation is coming to an end soon, if it's not there already. I've known that for a while, and there's never been any way I was going to hang around to be arrested and prosecuted. I had hoped the Brotherhood's lawyers would stop that happening, but now I believe there's only Manny, and no Brotherhood. And he's ditching us anyway. So that ain't gonna happen.

'Burke was going to be the icing on the cake, so far as the prosecution was concerned. It meant they could throw in a murder rap on top of everything else. Missing out on Burke has probably sealed it for us in Manny's eyes, and I believe he'll have washed his hands of us now.

'That'll be why he wanted us here in the first place. I never understood that. But he'll have wanted Zeman to get rid of us once we'd helped him get rid of the Podolsky woman. Her house would have been the perfect place for it to happen.

'Meanwhile, the attack on the cable that we had organised would go ahead. A perfect solution for him. All corners covered. Well, it didn't happen — yet! And it's not *going* to happen, if we play our cards right.'

Smith shook his head and said, 'That's a hell of a lot to take in.'

'Yeah. It's right, though.'

'So what can we do to turn it round? What's your thinking?'

'First, Jed, are you going to stick with me?'

'I guess,' Smith said with a shrug.

'If you want to walk away, feel free. Just go. I wouldn't blame you.'

'Where would I go? There's no place I could go. We've been together a long time, me and you. I'll stick with you.'

'Good,' Kravertz said with a nod. 'I hoped you would feel that way.'

'So what do we do?'

'To be honest with you, Jed, I've been planning on quitting anyway at some point, and I've made certain arrangements. No way was I going to hang around to the bitter end of KOSC. Initially, I'll go to South America. Argentina. It's safe there. You can come with me, if you fancy it?'

'South America, huh?' Smith said thoughtfully. 'I like the sound of that. What would we do there?'

'I'm already invested in a couple of businesses in Argentina. They would keep us busy enough for a while. Then we'd have to see what else we could find. There'll be opportunities. Before we set sail, though, we've got unfinished business right here in this city.'

'Oh?'

'First, we gotta get away from here before Zeman gets round to shooting us. Second, I want to see if we can find the Podolsky woman. I'm sure she'll be back in this city now, where the family is based, and I think I know where she'll be.'

'Where's that?'

'The Podolsky fortress that Zeman talked about. If we get lucky, we can do what he wanted to do all along.'

'What? Grab her, you mean?'

Kravertz nodded. 'It may not be possible, but it's a good idea and worth a shot. If we could pull it off, we could ransom her and sell her to the highest bidder. Then we would walk out of this city with something to cushion our new life over the water. What do you say?'

Smith thought for a few moments, and then nodded. 'It's a plan,' he said. 'Count me in. I've got nothing to go back to in the UK, anyway.'

'Good. I couldn't do it on my own.'

'So, we're partners now?'

'Partners.' Kravertz confirmed it with a grin. 'Now we've got to get out of here.'

A few minutes later the opportunity arose. Zeman wanted to talk to them. He said they had things to discuss.

'OK,' Kravertz said. 'I'm listening. So talk.'

Zeman stooped to sit down. That was when Smith, standing behind him, hit him hard on the head with a heavy piece of Bohemian glassware shaped like a tree trunk. Zeman collapsed in a heap.

Smith reached down and began rifling through Zeman's pockets. 'He usually keeps the car key on him.'

Kravertz nodded and waited anxiously.

'Found 'em!' Smith said triumphantly, holding up a small bunch of keys.

'Good man!'

'What now?' Smith asked.

'That's easy. Let's go!'

CHAPTER SEVENTY-FOUR

Podolsky House
14 December

'I can't fucking believe this,' Kravertz said, peering through his monocular. 'That's her!'

'The Podolsky woman?'

'Yeah. Right out in the open.'

Smith peered at the figure walking towards their car. 'Are you sure?'

'I am. Zeman showed me some photos of her.'

Smith wasn't sure, but he hadn't seen the photos, and he didn't have the eyepiece, either.

'Where did she come from?' he asked.

'Out of the Podolsky compound, or estate — whatever the hell they call it.'

'It seems weird, walking outside on her own like this.'

Kravertz nodded. 'Damned right, it is! And we're not gonna waste this opportunity. Get set! We'll grab her.'

CHAPTER SEVENTY-FIVE

It had taken him a while, but Henry had come back to me with some interesting extra information arising from his digging into KOSC and Kravertz.

'I'm surprised the various authorities haven't discovered who's behind Kravertz,' he'd said without preamble. 'Well, not really surprised. They're all pretty useless in my opinion. And this proves it. How long has that investigation been going on into KOSC? How many months, years? About . . .'

'Cut to the chase, Henry, if you don't mind. I'm a bit busy here.'

'Like that, is it?' he'd said stiffly.

'It is, I'm afraid.'

He took a few moments to indulge in a fit of coughing inspired by his cigarette addiction. He used to smoke Capstan Extra Strength, and it showed. God knows what he used these days, given how much the smoking scene had changed. Illegal imports, probably, from somewhere like Azerbaijan or Tajikistan.

'Back on the cigs, Henry?'

I got a growled response that made me smile. Henry wasn't best pleased.

'I bet Maggie doesn't know,' I added, only just managing to forbear from giving him unwanted advice.

'I've cut down a bit,' he managed.

'Good. I'm glad to hear it. You'll be better for it. Now, what were you going to tell me about Kravertz's backers?'

'Just one backer, I think. It's a guy called Kurt Mannheim. Megabucks is his background.'

'What part of Germany does he live in?'

'Las Vegas, although he has interests and properties still in his ancestral homeland.'

'Mafia?'

'No. He's a one-man band, but he's as big as most of that lot. Maybe bigger.'

'Casinos, of course?'

'Casinos, as well. Plus all sorts of other legitimate businesses. But he's never given up the activities and industries that got him his start in life. He's a very shady character, and very successful with it. A good match with Kravertz.'

It had become increasingly clear that Kravertz did have a backer, or backers. A big offshore business like KOSC isn't something you can start without major money to put at risk, and Kravertz seemed to have come from nowhere. Nobody had found evidence that he personally had that kind of wealth.

This was clear not only to me and Leon. Even various branches of UK government had been onto this for some time, notwithstanding Henry's unflattering opinion of them. That was what had led to the official inquiry into KOSC.

I wondered if Kravertz had come to the realisation, especially after Jamie's desertion, that the inquiry, and his time at the helm of KOSC, was fast coming to an end. That could explain the planned attack on the new interconnector. Maybe he, or his backer, had decided it would be a good and rewarding idea to sign off with a flourish, and make a pile of money at the same time.

'So you think this Mannheim guy funded KOSC and put Kravertz in charge of it?'

'Yeah.' Henry paused before delivering his damning verdict in more detail. 'It's a big money-spinner, all that North Sea work — decommissioning and dismantling oil and gas rigs, and all that. It also took a lot of money to start up. But KOSC got in on the ground floor, and they'll have done pretty well out of it.

'All went well until Her Majesty's Customs and Revenue, et al, started their investigation, wanting to know where KOSC's set-up money had come from and who really owned the company. Things started deteriorating then, and the business with Jamie accelerated the process. It looks now like they don't have far to go.'

'Nor has Kravertz, in that case.'

'Exactly.'

'Mannheim should be OK, though?'

'Oh, I would think so, wouldn't you? Big money talks — and walks. The really big guys are hard to catch — so long as they don't fiddle their income tax returns.'

I smiled at that. Capone had illustrated how even the biggest can be brought down to earth.

'Well, thanks, Henry. That's all very interesting.'

'Isn't it? How's Jamie?'

'Good. OK, thanks.'

'Can I talk to him?'

'Of course. He's not here right now, but I'll get him to call you.'

* * *

Afterwards, I told Leon what I'd learned from Henry. His opinion was the same as mine.

'It seems like Kravertz decided to make a last wedge of money, and then pull out with a bang and disappear,' he said.

I nodded agreement. I couldn't have put it better myself.

Leon frowned thoughtfully for a moment, and then said, 'So it's Mannheim behind him. I know that name somehow. I've heard it mentioned.' He paused and added, 'Ask your friend, Henry, if Mannheim has any interest in electricity.'

'That's an idea. I'll get straight back to him.'

* * *

I called Henry back and asked the question Leon had raised.

'Can you do some digging on that, Henry?'

'No need. I know the answer already. It's yes. He is involved in electricity. In supply, not generation. He's a broker, one of those guys that holds a product until someone wants it badly, and then they send it to whoever will pay the most.'

'Just like they do with tankers full of oil and gas?'

'Exactly. All legitimate and above board. Healthy capitalism in action, fine-tuning demand and supply. No different to what they do in the City of London, moving grain and minerals around the market place. Futures trading, they call it there.'

'And legitimate, unless or until the broker starts interfering with the supply train?' I suggested.

'You've got it.'

'Thanks, Henry.'

'Does that help explain anything?'

'It sure does. Now we know what's going on.' I ended the call before Henry could press me to tell him what that was. Now was not the time to go into all that with him.

* * *

'Wouldn't it be good,' I'd said to Leon, 'if we could bring both of them down — Kravertz and Mannheim?'

'Indeed it would,' Leon admitted with a grin. 'Let me know how you think we could do that!'

CHAPTER SEVENTY-SIX

I decided Olga had the right idea and headed outside myself for some peace and quiet, and some fresh air. It had been an exhilarating but exhausting time lately. The Podolskys lived like this all the time, but I couldn't. Already I was hankering to be back home at Risky Point. Poor Olga, though. Where would she go now?

More to the point, where was she right now? I had expected to see her in the garden, but she wasn't in sight when I went outside. That seemed strange. I spun round, looking for her, and caught a glimpse of someone going out through the entrance in the distance.

Olga? Surely not? I couldn't be sure at this distance, but if it was I didn't like the idea. Not unaccompanied.

I broke into a run for the gateway. If it wasn't Olga, there was no problem. But if it was, she couldn't afford to be going out of the Podolsky precinct unprotected, not after everything that had been going on lately.

It was Olga.

As soon as I was out through the gates, I saw her sauntering along the footpath beside the tree-lined road, seemingly without a care in the world. I had to challenge that.

But it was like a re-run of the incident with Jamie. As I started to run, a car drew up alongside her. A man jumped out and grabbed her, and then the driver came round the car to help him.

Olga kicked and screamed. The man holding her punched her in the stomach to shut her up. She dropped to the ground. The man who had hit her straightened up and turned to meet me as I charged towards them.

A big man with a ginger beard. Jed Smith! Not that it mattered who it was.

He pulled out a gun. I hit him before he could bring it to bear on me. We both went to the ground, me on top. I grabbed hold of his gun arm with both my hands and put up with the blows he delivered with his free hand.

He was strong. I needed both hands to hold the gun away. We turned and scrambled, kicked and punched, rolled and ground each other into the dirt. Then the gun was fired, and his grip slackened. I tore the gun out of his hand. But it was another moment or two before I realised he had stopped fighting.

Still on the floor, I rolled on to my back and pointed the gun at the second man. I was met by him pointing a gun at me. Neither of us fired. Perhaps we both realised sub-consciously that if one gun fired, the other would, too. Automatically. Reflex. Or whatever.

Keeping the gun trained on him, I scrambled to my feet and straightened up. He was unmoving. A quick glance sideways told me so was Jed Smith. The difference between them was that one of them was dead.

'Olga?'

'I'm all right,' she gasped, from where she still lay on the ground.

'Kravertz?' I said then. 'Have I got that right?'

He just stared hard at me.

'And who might you be?' he demanded after a moment.

I ignored the question. I wasn't in the mood for conversation. My mind was spinning, racing through the permutations, trying to decide what to do next.

I could shoot, and I might get away with it. Hit him and grab his gun before he fired back. Hope his reflexes were not so sharp. Hope he missed me. Maybe. But there was a lot of hoping in there.

His understanding of the situation was probably the same as my own. Neither of us held an advantage here. Neither of us could be sure of coming out of an exchange of gunfire unharmed.

'Drop your gun!' I instructed. 'Drop it, and live.'

He just sneered at me.

Keeping my gun trained on Kravertz, I kicked Smith to make sure. No response. Dead. Because of that one, single, accidental gunshot.

I saw Kravertz's eyes wander towards Smith's body. That gave me a chance. I leapt at Kravertz, taking the risk, and seized his gun hand and forced it back and away from me. Then I kneed him in the groin and he sagged, giving both the gun and the struggle up.

He wasn't a strong man. Not like Smith. I stepped back and waited for him to recover. By then, other possibilities were crowding in on my thoughts. It didn't have to end in more gunfire. That wasn't the only option, I had realised. Recent discussions with Henry and with Leon had come to mind, and with them the name Mannheim.

'Olga, can you walk?'

'I think so,' she said hesitantly, as she clambered to her feet.

'In a minute, I might ask you to start walking back to the gateway to get help. But, first, I'm going to see if Mr Kravertz is minded to do a deal with us.'

CHAPTER SEVENTY-SEVEN

'A deal? What you got in mind?' Kravertz asked. 'Money?'

'In part,' I told him. 'Money to rebuild Miss Podolsky's house. That will be one million, in sterling. As for myself, my main interest is in seeing Jamie Burke being allowed to live his life without having to keep looking over his shoulder to see if you're coming for him.'

I could see him thinking seriously about it. As a man without a gun, and being a man facing one, he didn't have a lot of options. Also, I guessed he had run out of people who could help him. Why else would he be here?

'Just you and Smith,' I said, glancing around. 'What happened to your Czech friends?'

He shrugged. 'There was a parting of the ways.'

'After you didn't catch us in Kámen? A disagreement, perhaps?'

No response, which told its own story.

'You going to lay out the deal?' he asked. 'Or do we just stand here until someone sees us and calls the cops?'

He looked terrible. I knew I probably did, as well, but Kravertz didn't look like a man who owned a big offshore company, or any other kind of business. His clothes were torn and dirtied, his face scratched and bruised, and his hair looked as if someone had set fire to it. All to the good, so far as I was concerned. I needed him to have every disadvantage possible.

'OK,' I said. 'Let me spell it out for you. But maybe we should all get in the car first. It's been a long couple of days, and we're probably all feeling a bit tired.'

After I'd checked it out to be sure nobody else was lurking in there, Olga got in the back. I sat Kravertz behind the steering wheel, and took the front passenger seat myself.

'You're in a very poor position,' I told him. 'You're an intelligent man, so you'll have grasped that. Your main interest right now will be in getting away from here, and out of this country. Right?'

'Get on with it,' he snapped.

'Option one for us is we take you back into the Podolsky estate, hold you there and hand you over to the cops when they come. I don't like that one very much, because it won't guarantee Jamie's future. As I said, that's my main concern now.

'Option two is the deal. We let you go, to make your own way out of here. Perhaps you could contact Mr Mannheim and get him to come and collect you?'

He didn't say anything.

'Before that happens, though, we want a bank transfer of the funds needed to rebuild the house. We should be able to do that from right here. Also, I want a guarantee that any hit on Jamie Burke that you've organised is cancelled, and that from now on he will be left alone. Meet those two conditions, my friend, and you're free to go.'

It was a gamble, for all sorts of reasons, but I didn't want to shoot him in cold blood, and I thought it a better option than turning him over to the Czech authorities. If we did that, lawyers could intervene and stop extradition, and maybe even get him released, if only on bail. Then he would disappear, Jamie would be no better off, and Kravertz and Mannheim would both still be in play.

My thinking was that Kravertz no longer had anything going for him now, and badly needed Mannheim to come and help him. Mannheim would surely do that, in order to help himself. Kravertz, loose or in custody, would be a problem, and a threat to him.

I was also thinking something else, and I had to be sure Olga had meant what she said when she told me she respected my judgement. For this to work, I needed her to follow my lead and play a part.

'Olga,' I said, turning round to look her in the eye, 'are you OK with this? The bank transfer, and everything?'

'Yes,' she said promptly. 'That will be the perfect solution. For the house and for Jamie.'

'How about you?' I asked, turning back to Kravertz.

'Let's get it done,' he said briskly. 'But how can I guarantee to leave off pursuing Burke? What would satisfy you? More money?'

I shook my head. 'No.'

Now we got to the tricky part.

'I'll take your word for it.'

He nodded, and managed not to look surprised.

'Just one thing,' I added. 'I want you to know that if you renege on the deal, and reactivate a hit on Jamie, you'll then be in the same position as he is now.

'We'll come for you. And we'll do that because nothing will be more important than that to the Podolsky family, who have virtually unlimited resources to commit to an unending hunt for you. Hiding, plastic surgery or whatever else you can come up with will not prevent us finding you.'

'No need to worry about that,' he assured me. 'I'll have much bigger issues to deal with than Jamie Burke. Let me leave here, and you can tell Jamie he needn't worry any more about me.'

CHAPTER SEVENTY-EIGHT

How it played out was like this. Olga gave Kravertz the details of the bank account she wanted the money for the house paid into, and he got busy with his phone. That took a few minutes.

Meanwhile, Olga took out her own phone and got ready to check that the payment had been made. There's no waiting around with high-end accounts, like these, unlike the kind that most of us have. Transactions happen fast.

Olga knew that I knew she didn't need the money, but I knew that she knew what this was really about. What we were doing was making it possible, later, to see where Kravertz's money was coming from. It might not be easy to do, but I'd seen Olga in action before and I had great faith in her capabilities.

I was less confident about the value of Kravertz's assurances with regard to Jamie. Not confident at all, in fact. The word of someone like him is worthless. My threat of follow-up if he reneged on the deal might help keep him in line, but I doubted that as well. It didn't matter. What I wanted was to bring Kravertz and Mannheim together. If I could do that, there was a chance that somehow they could both be brought down.

Legal processes were unlikely to accomplish that, for all the reasons I listed earlier: money, lawyers, courts, national sovereignties. Different jurisdictions would be involved, and it would be particularly difficult if one or other of the pair sought refuge in a country without relevant extradition treaties.

Even before that, though, how on earth could legally convincing evidence ever be brought to bear on them, and how long would it take? Squads of highly paid lawyers would do their utmost to make sure that never happened. So Jamie would remain at risk. I didn't want that. Targeting the two principals directly and bringing them together seemed a more promising option. Hell, maybe they would even shoot each other! Who knew?

Although Kravertz wouldn't know it yet, the attempt to sabotage the interconnector had failed. Mannheim would probably know that, though, and if he didn't, he would very very soon. It was very likely that he would see Kravertz as a liability, one he needed to get rid of fast.

For his part, Kravertz had been around long enough to know how things worked in the circles in which he moved. He was at risk now and needed to look after himself — if necessary, by being proactive. But without passport or wallet, of which I relieved him, and generally in a bit of a mess, he would need help to get out of the country and onto safer territory. Why not Mannheim?

It was probably too much to hope that they would finish each other off, but you never knew. Anyway, the deal I'd offered Kravertz had been the best thing I could come up with at the time. I'd talk to Leon about it. Then we would wait and see how it played out.

'The money has been transferred,' Olga announced.

'That was quick,' I said, surprised.

'It is why we use this bank.'

Kravertz came awake. 'So what now?' he asked.

'If it were me, I would call Mannheim and get him to come for you in a private plane. That's the best way for you to get out of the country, especially if your Czech pals are looking for you.'

He thought for a moment and then nodded, and got busy again on his phone. The way I saw it, he didn't have much choice. A reply came so quickly that I guessed he had activated some sort of standing emergency protocol.

'It's done,' he said.

'Right.'

I nodded to Olga, who got out of the car.

'You can take Smith with you,' I said to Kravertz. 'After all, he's been with you all along.'

He didn't seem bothered one way or the other, and helped me put the body in the boot.

'You're free to go now,' I told him.

CHAPTER SEVENTY-NINE

Olga and I returned to the residence and brought Leon up to date. He was probably annoyed with Olga for going outside alone, but wisely kept his thoughts to himself. She had enough on her mind, and to do.

'Right,' he said crisply. 'You did well, both of you. It is possible that the end is in sight for them both, Kravertz and Mannheim. Get to work, Olga! Let's see if we can make it happen.'

'The bank account first, I think,' Olga said thoughtfully. 'While I'm doing that, Leon, can you have someone download the telecoms scanner?'

I already knew all messages and calls flying through the ether within a certain distance of their boundary were collected. That was something that had underlain my thinking when talking to Kravertz.

'Josef is here at the moment,' Leon said. 'I'll ask him to identify calls and messages to and from Kravertz.'

Turning to me, as Olga left, Leon said, 'It will be interesting to see what's in that bank account of his.'

I agreed. 'Yes. Very interesting. I figured that having to make a payment like that, he wouldn't use a personal account. It would have to be one with plenty in it. Maybe even the KOSC account — and not the petty cash account, either!'

'Well, let's see what Olga comes up with. In the meantime, you can tell me what your thinking was when you let Kravertz go. Why not just shoot him?'

'Not my style, Leon. You know that. Smith is enough to have on my conscience, although that was an accident. Anyway, don't you like my plan?'

'Not my style!' he said with a grin. 'But what were you thinking? Knowing you, it wouldn't be anything straightforward.'

'Is that a vote of confidence?'

'Depends on what you tell me now.'

'Well, it was the best I could come up with in the circumstances. It would have been easy to hold on to Kravertz and hope to have him arrested, but would the police have done that on our say-so? Even if they had, would he have been kept in custody when he had an army of lawyers clamouring for him to be released? Once released, he'd have been out of the country, and no doubt gone underground, in five minutes.

'Also, you and I agreed that it wasn't only Kravertz we wanted to take down. We wanted his backer, Mannheim, as well. This way, if it works out, we'll be bringing both of them together, which will be a start. It gives us the opportunity to do more, or for something else to happen.'

'Hmm.'

Leon mused for a moment or two, and then said, 'You were thinking . . . what — that they might eliminate each other?'

'That would be nice, wouldn't it? Well, they might. It's always possible.' I shrugged, and added, 'I just thought something might turn up.'

That sounded a bit lame now that I was trying to explain myself free of the stress and excitement of the moment, but I persevered.

'In the next day or so, if he hasn't already picked up on it, Mannheim is going to discover that the plan to sabotage the interconnector hasn't worked. With everything else going on as well — the investigation, the murder enquiry, et cetera — that's when he's going to see Kravertz as a liability and a danger.

'It will be clear he needs to be shut up, and got rid of, before he can say or do anything that will bring Mannheim himself down. So it will suit him to come for Kravertz. He can't just abandon him here, in case he gets picked up by the Czech authorities and tells them what he knows in order to help himself.

'Kravertz is likely to come to the same conclusion about where he stands with Mannheim, and take steps to try to stop his own elimination happening. Remember, too, that if Olga is successful, Kravertz will have lost a lot of money, as well as the business he was supposed to own. He might not be actually "skint", as we say in the north country, but his resources will be much depleted. That should encourage him to take bold action in his own interest.'

'Diabolical thinking, Frank!' Leon grinned and added, 'I thought you would have something in mind. Oh, to be present when the two of them meet!'

'Fingers crossed,' I said.

CHAPTER EIGHTY

It was Josef who reported back first. A studious-looking young man, I had no doubt even before he spoke that he would be on top of his game. Leon didn't recruit duffers. And so it proved.

'We picked up a number of communications,' he said in American-accented English. 'SMS and phone calls, one or two emails. Everything sent and received within a ten-kilometre range.'

Very few had anything to do with Kravertz, but Josef gave us what we had wanted to hear.

'Someone is to make their way to Vaclav Havel Airport by 19.00, this evening. They are to go to the terminal dealing only with private flights, where they will be collected.'

There was a little more, but that was the essential message.

'Thank you, Josef,' Leon said thoughtfully. 'That is what we wanted to know.'

As Josef departed, Leon nodded with satisfaction, and said, 'Now we know where things stand.'

I agreed. Things were going well so far.

Leon frowned and added, 'I will send Lenka there to find out more.'

'She will fly there?'

'Of course.'

Of course she would. Lenka's helicopter was used like a taxi.

'Then what?' I asked.

He smiled. 'Then we will see, Frank, and decide if there is more we can do.'

A typically Delphic observation.

* * *

A little later Olga appeared, looking well-worn and weary, but triumphant all the same.

'It is a big account in the Cayman Islands,' she said without preamble. 'Thirty million there, in sterling. I believe it is for the KOSC business, and not a Kravertz personal account.'

Wow! I couldn't help thinking. That was a hell of a big bank balance.

'You got into it?' Leon asked.

She nodded.

'And?'

'And I have emptied it. All the money has been transferred out.'

'Excellent!' Leon thrust a triumphant fist into the air.

'Good. He's going to be badly strapped for cash,' I mused.

'Perhaps not,' Leon cautioned, 'if this is not his own personal account. But he will be very angry, I think, and Mannheim even more so.'

That was what I thought, too. One way or another, the walls were closing in on the pair of them fast.

CHAPTER EIGHTY-ONE

It didn't work out quite as I hoped. Mainly because the Podolskys, all three of them, joined the action and shaped the outcome.

I should have thought something was up when I saw Olga apparently briefing Lenka about something just before the latter left the house to fire up her chopper. But there were many possible explanations for that. I was curious, but not pressingly so.

Then Olga was gone, too. That did interest me rather more, and at least, Leon did tell me something about that.

'She's tracking Kravertz's vehicle,' he said airily.

'Oh? Why?'

'We want to see where he goes.'

Fair enough, if puzzling.

'How can she do that?' I asked belatedly, and even more puzzled.

'On her computer.'

'Tracking his car on it?'

'Yes. She put a tracker beacon under the back seat.'

'She happened to have one with her?'

He just nodded.

'Hmm. She didn't tell me anything about that.'

'You had enough to think about, Frank,' Leon said in a kindly tone.

* * *

Once again, I seemed to be the only one who wasn't busy. So I went to talk to Jamie, who had been installed in one of the bedrooms.

'Resting again?' I said with a grin. 'I wondered what you were doing.'

'Oh, you know how it is, Frank. When you've got a bad leg, you have to take it easy, don't you?'

'True.' I squinted at him thoughtfully, feeling my leg was being pulled a bit, though not too badly. 'How are you doing?'

'OK, thanks. Pretty good, actually. But I can't put weight on it yet. I'm told I need to wait a bit longer, or I'll be in trouble.'

I nodded. That sounded about right. No point ignoring the medical advice.

'So what do you want to do now you're a free man again, Jamie, now the threat from KOSC is over? Go home with me in a day or two?'

He shook his head. 'Sorry, Frank. I'm already booked up. I'm going off somewhere with someone called Charles, another injured man, apparently.'

I was a bit taken aback by that.

'Oh? Well, I do know who Charles is. But you're going somewhere with him? Where to?'

'Switzerland, apparently. We're both going to a sanatorium there, to convalesce some more. Leon arranged it, and I quite fancy that.'

I felt quite faint. *Nobody tells me anything*, I couldn't help thinking.

'Just one thing, Frank. Can you let Jenny know I'm all right, and I'll be home in another week or two?'

Still feeling faint, I said, 'So that's still on, is it? Your relationship with her?'

'Oh, yes. She's the girl for me, all right.'

Like I said, nobody tells me anything.

* * *

A couple of hours later Olga joined Leon and me as we sat nursing a beer while we watched a Czech news channel.

Leon turned the sound off and turned to Olga expectantly, it seemed to me.

'Kravertz didn't make it,' she said calmly. 'Is that beer you are both drinking?'

'It is,' Leon said. 'Would you like one?'

'Thank you. I think I would now,' she said.

While Leon busied himself at a fridge, I asked Olga what she had meant about Kravertz.

'His car crashed on the way to Prague,' she said with a shrug. 'He didn't survive.'

I was astonished, even though I probably shouldn't have been.

'It was on the news?' I asked, thinking we hadn't seen it.

'Not yet,' she said. 'But I'm sure it will be.'

But Olga knew already? That was when I began to understand.

'So what happened? Do you know that, as well?'

'Tyre blowout, Lenka told me.'

'I see. And Lenka happened to be close by, of course?'

'Yes. She had been following Kravertz's car.'

'Aided by the tracker you installed? And possibly contributing to the . . . the accident?'

Olga gave me a smile that meant a lot. 'Lenka is a trained sniper, as well as a pilot, remember?' she said gently.

I sighed heavily and said, 'It would have been nice to have been kept in the loop, Olga, after all we've been through together.'

'It's not your style, Frank. Isn't that what you told Leon?' she asked with another disarming smile.

* * *

Much later there was another accident. This one was reported on the national news. A small private plane had crashed not long after take-off from Vaclav Havel Airport. The pilot, who was also the owner, had died in the crash. There were no passengers, or other crew members. Engine failure was provisionally believed to be the reason, but that needed to be confirmed by an official investigation, which was likely to take some time.

'Well, Leon,' I said, understanding full well now. 'That about concludes our business, I believe.'

'Yes, it does,' he agreed with a nod. 'I know what your feelings are likely to be, Frank, but we Podolskys feel a little differently. Actually, so do my friends in the Admiralty. They are very pleased with the outcome.'

'Really?'

He nodded. 'They are happy to have someone do for them what they cannot do themselves.'

And so the world, I thought wearily. Not my style, perhaps, but in a way, the outcome satisfied me, too. The Podolskys had got things done once again. And I had helped them.

'Something happened, Frank,' Leon pointed out. 'Your plan worked.'

'Yes. You're right.' I thought for a moment and then added, 'I'm not unhappy about it, either.'

'Good,' Leon said briskly. 'Neither am I.'

We shook hands then and called it a day. It had been another long one.

CHAPTER EIGHTY-TWO

Before I left Prague, I had a last word with the person I had come here to help.

'What about you, Olga? What will you do now?'

'Oh, there is always plenty of work for me, Frank. But I will take a little time out for a while. I must, if I am to rebuild the house in Kámen.'

I smiled. Then I realised she meant it.

'Rebuild the house? Really?'

'Of course. You obtained the money to enable me to do that. But I would have done it anyway. Always, I try to leave things better than when I found them.'

I thought of what would be left there. A heap of smouldering ash. But I knew she meant it. She would rebuild it, as she had done with Chesters.

'As it was?' I asked.

'Of course.'

'Exactly?'

'Exactly, but better.'

I smiled again. As I've said more than once before, Olga is special, a special kind of person.

'And thank you, Frank, for everything else you and Jamie did for me. It is difficult to find the words,' she said with a frown, 'but I would have been lost without you coming to support me. I want you to know how much I appreciate what you have done for me.'

'No need to say more, Olga. We made a good team, didn't we?'

Then she gave me that special smile that not many get to see.

* * *

As soon as I got home, Jimmy Mack came to the door to welcome me.

'Good trip, Frank?'

I nodded. 'It was OK, thanks.'

'Well, I'm glad you're back. Bill Peart has been round here every day nearly, muttering about when you two are going to be able to go fishing again. He's wearing me out.'

'I'll call him. And put him out of his misery.'

'Good. Did Jamie come back with you?'

'No. He's decided to go to Switzerland for a week or two before he comes home. I think he's got a taste for foreign travel.'

'Wouldn't suit me.'

'No, Jim,' I said with a grin. 'I don't suppose it would. And right now, I don't want any more of it for a while, either. I'm very pleased to be home.'

* * *

'Morning, Bill. How are you?'

'Oh, you're back, are you?'

'Just.'

'Successful trip? Enjoyable?'

'Yes, and no. You know how it goes sometimes.'

'Good weather and cheap wine not all it's cracked up to be, eh?'

I chuckled, thinking, *If only he knew!*

'Burke with you?'

'No. He's decided to stay away a bit longer.'

'Well, it doesn't really matter. He's not needed now, not urgently, anyway.'

'Oh?'

'KOSC has collapsed and Kravertz is dead, killed in a car crash. So everything's on hold here until the legalities of that lot get sorted out. But I can tell you more about that when we get out fishing. Still interested in getting the boat out?'

'I am.'

'When?'

'How about tomorrow?'

'Suits me.'

I smiled when I put the phone down, and wondered what I would tell him. Not much, probably. What happens in Prague stays in Prague. That still seemed the best policy.

THE END

THE JOFFE BOOKS STORY

We began in 2014 when Jasper agreed to publish his mum's much-rejected romance novel and it became a bestseller.

Since then we've grown into the largest independent publisher in the UK. We're extremely proud to publish some of the very best writers in the world, including Joy Ellis, Faith Martin, Caro Ramsay, Helen Forrester, Simon Brett and Robert Goddard. Everyone at Joffe Books loves reading and we never forget that it all begins with the magic of an author telling a story.

We are proud to publish talented first-time authors, as well as established writers whose books we love introducing to a new generation of readers.

We won Trade Publisher of the Year at the Independent Publishing Awards in 2023 and Best Publisher Award in 2024 at the People's Book Prize. We have been shortlisted for Independent Publisher of the Year at the British Book Awards for the last five years, and were shortlisted for the Diversity and Inclusivity Award at the 2022 Independent Publishing Awards. In 2023 we were shortlisted for Publisher of the Year at the RNA Industry Awards, and in 2024 we were shortlisted at the CWA Daggers for the Best Crime and Mystery Publisher.

We built this company with your help, and we love to hear from you, so please email us about absolutely anything bookish at feedback@joffebooks.com.

If you want to receive free books every Friday and hear about all our new releases, join our mailing list here: www.joffebooks.com/freebooks.

And when you tell your friends about us, just remember: it's pronounced Joffe as in coffee or toffee!

www.ingramcontent.com/pod-product-compliance
Ingram Content Group UK Ltd.
Pitfield, Milton Keynes, MK11 3LW, UK
UKHW021136040225
4431UKWH00008B/76

9 781835 269817